The Momma's Boy Project.

I0692989

Alexandria R. West

The Momma's Boy Project

Suave Publishing

Copyright ©2009 by Alexandria R. West

ISBN-13: 978-0-578-01202-5

"I can do all things through Christ who strengthens me".

Philippians 4:13

This book is dedicated first and foremost to my parents, Theresa and Ronald who raised me to believe that I can do anything with hard work and dedication and who have always loved me unconditionally-even if I sometimes act a little uppity and bourgeois. It is also dedicated to my best friend Tim and my 4 wonderful children- Naiyelle, Malcolm, Quentin and Zavier who had patience to see me through this writing journey; bringing me drinks and food to my office and understood even if it meant that I had to miss part of a football, basketball or field hockey game or keep you up because I was typing well after midnight.

I also dedicate this book to my other parents mom Sharon Choice and Darrell who always told me to do what I know was right and my niece Jasmine who gave me pep talks and told me jokes when I thought I would never complete this book and who always made me keep our girl time- by going to Starbucks for frappucinos and going shopping at King of Prussia.

To my dear and longtime friend Tyese, thanks for all of the morning chat fests on the way to work, the trips to Franklin Mills (running from foxes), and all of the girls nights out- husband de-stress outings that gave me me faith that I would complete this journey as well as the mantra- "We need to start something of our own". Thanks for being an honest and loyal friend-even if it means talking to me when I'm being really moody!

This is also dedicated to my two guardian Angels my grandmother Josephine, and my sister girl Dana whose spirit lives in my heart and through her daughter Jasmine everyday- I miss you Dana.

To my little big brother Eric- "Problems, Difficulties, Obstacles- Need Help? Always know that I have your back and love you unconditionally, keep doing your grown man thing and I am <u>always</u> proud of you. Thanks for being the strength that only a little big brother can be.

To my grandmother Delores, my mother, my aunts Pat and Joan, my son's godmother Marcia, my sisters Celeste and Taijuanna and my great aunt Lovonia, thanks for showing me what it means to be strong women through tough times. You all have enlightened me on what it truly means to weather the storm.

To Brandon "B" Crystian (Pittsburgh), Uncle Braheem, Mark Simmons, Weston, Robert Triebig and Alonzo Coates as well as those who took the time to be a brother or father figure to me, thanks for all of the insight into a man's mind and thanks for just being good friends to me- And they say Men and Women can't just be friends!

To Kimmie, Niese, Jessica, Jodi Della Barba, Aleandra, Davida, Cassandra, Joneen and Tabitha, thank you for all of the encouragement, anecdotes , re-reads and help with editing. I don't think I would have been able to get this down to a science without all of your feedback I love you all.

To all of my sisters- especially my FAVORITE little sister (you know who you are!) -"We Fly" - thanks for the encouragement. This is your success as it is mines.

Lastly, to all of the people who turned their backs on me and weren't willing to weather the storm with me as friends with a lame excuse as we just grew apart- Peace and Blessings to all of you and like my one of my favorites rappers Kool Moe Dee once said- "How you like me now!"

If I left anyone out, please attribute it to my head and not my heart! - Alex

Prologue

James opened the door to his studio apartment and hung his keys on the key holder. He walked over to the answering machine and pushed play so that he could listen to the message. "You have 3 messages waiting", the machine chimed.

"Beep- James this is mommy please call me, I need to talk to you as soon as get this message.

James sighed; he wondered how many times did she leave that message today. His mother knew that today was the day that he went to court to finalize all the details of his legal separation from his wife of 10 years. He could not deal with whatever problem was going on at his mom's right know. He was depressed. As much as he tried to get Mikki to see that a separation was not what they needed because he loved her and the children so much, she just did not want to hear what he was saying. The longer he lived in his studio apartment, the more he just could not stand being without her and their 5 children. He missed waking up and being part of the morning routine with Mikki; he just missed being in his home. And right know there was nothing he could do about it.

He pushed the button to hear the next message;

"James this is your mother, I need you to call me when you get a chance it is very important".

James sighed and listened to the last message-

"Hi Daddy, this is Shannon and Skylar, we just wanted to call and say good morning and that we love you bye- oh! We almost forgot, Steven, Scott and Jason say they love you too".

After James heard that he just wanted to cry. He decided right then and there that he was going to do whatever he needed to get his family back and by any means necessary.

Mikki

Mikki pulled into the garage and turned off the car. She walked up the steps and pushed the button to close the garage door and went in the house. After the day's proceedings, she was tired, but she knew that she had to get herself together to face her mother who watched the twins and Jason for her while she ventured into Philly to go to court. She was trying to be brave because she had 5 children all under the age of 8 and she was now going to be the sole parent for a while. It was her idea to separate from James but she could not put up with his double life and not putting their family first. James was good man, no doubt, but for as long as she could remember, his mother and her family always stood in the way of theirs and she just got tired of it after awhile.

She remembered the last argument they had about it like it was yesterday. "James, we have plans today, I hope you did not forget?"

" I know Mikki, we are going to Alex's cookout, but you know that they never have the food ready on time so , I told my mom that I would take her shopping early and then you , the kids and I can head over to Alex's and enjoy ourselves."

"Why would you do that?" "I mean, we had these plans for months now and you know that Scott and Steven wanted to be there early so that they could get in the pool with Marcus."

"The boys will have enough time to play with Marcus if we get there after 3". "I promised".

"Promise, promise, promise - we should not have to compromise our time or for that matter rearrange our time, for your mother! What do your brother's do for her nothing! She has a husband for that matter and if anything goes wrong, who does she call, you James! Did you forget that I am your wife and we have children that want to spend quality time with you?"

"Oh, Mikki here you go with the drama again! You knew when we began dating that I helped my mother and you said it yourself that it was noble that I helped my mother out. Now the drama queen can't stand it if we can't go to her friend's house early for a cookout and sit around and not be able to eat because the food is not ready! Please spare me the drama. I am helping my mother out, she is my mother, she will always be my mother and it is not going to kill you if we rearrange our plans and go a little late. So deal with it!", and he stormed out of the house.

Mikki thought to herself, that was the last argument that we had about his mother because the following Monday, she told James that she wanted to be separated and by the time he came home from work she had changed the locks on their house and went to her lawyers office and had him served with papers that afternoon when he was on his way to pick up Scott and Steven for basketball practice.

Mikki shut the door to the mud room and into her kitchen. Her mom was fast asleep in the family room on the couch with the twins and Jason was stretched out on their blankets on the floor. Mikki smiled and put the blanket over her mother and went upstairs to change her clothes.

"Yo! Mike come on man, I want to make sure that we get a good spot to see all the honeys at the Black Expo!" " I'm coming man, hold your horses, I need to make sure that my fade is nice and that the ladies see my waves and how nice they are laying without using any of that texturizing mess that some other brotha's use."

"Very funny, man- but come on, you know for sure that I am not going to this concert to hear After 7 sing. I heard that Chante Moore is a good singer, but I have never seen her in person so it is definitely, a lady watching nite". "James, I am surprised that after your fling with that girl in Virginia, that you would even be about that tonight".

"Look, let's not talk about Tammy, anyway that jawn got away with my $500 glasses and some of my nice gear and to top it all off she was crazy and decided she was going to snap on me because of my moms. She was a looney one and she had to go!"

The two best friends headed for the front door of Mike's apartment and jumped into James black Nissan. James started up the car while Mike admired the clean interior and new sound system. They drove from Mike's apartment and parked near 39th and Spruce streets. They walked down Spruce Street towards 38th and walked over 38th street until they got to Civic Center Boulevard and walked towards the Civic Center were the Black Expo was being held.

"Yo, James, there appears to be a plethora of ladies out here tonight!" "I see, I see". When they got in the civic center they walked to their seats and realized that they had the best seats in the house, they were six rows from the stage and because After 7 was the main act, most of the seats in those first six rows, were mainly women. James took in the scenery and decided that he was going to get some phone numbers tonite.

"Hey, Mike, Hey James", they both heard from behind them. They both turned around to see Jasmine one of the Kappa Sweethearts that they knew from Temple. "Hey Jaz wassup?" they said in unison.

"Nothing much, just here to see After 7 with a bunch of my friends". Mike put his arm around Jasmine and asked her to introduce him to her friends. Jasmine smiled and introduced them both to Serena, Andrea and Michelle. "These are my best friends growing up who also happen to be Kappa Sweethearts from Del State as well as my sorors because we all pledged Delta the same year".

"Well, well, well", James said, "It is nice to meet you all because, any Kappa Sweethearts are friends of mine". The lights in the Civic Center blinked as a warning for everyone that the show was about to start. "There is a party at Houston Hall after this, so we'll see you guys over there afterwards, Jaz", Mike said. "That's a bet we'll see you over there.

"James is your brother, deejaying the party?" "Yes, you know it", James answered, "so you know that party is going to be off the hook!"

They enjoyed the show and James was pleasantly surprised that Chante Moore could not only sing, but she had a great body and the dress that she had on would make a blind man sing her praises. They left the concert and headed up Civic Center towards Spruce street and walked over to Houston hall where James brother Chris was deejaying the college party. They paid to get in and headed over to the deejay booth were Chris was surrounded by some of James and Mike's fraternity brothers and a lot of college women.

"Wassup, Chris, how you living?" "Yo, bro, I'm chillin' and I this party has a lot of women up in here!" Please man, most of these women are babies and you know that." "Well, just chill and enjoy the party". "True dat, man".

James sat on the stage behind the deejay booth and just let his eyes wander around the room. He watched the fraternities and sororities party walk around Houston hall having a good time. Just then three young ladies who were coming into the party caught his eye. One was about 6'3 and she definitely had to be a basketball player with the gazelle like neck and legs. The other was about 5'5" with DD breast and her hair styled short like Toni Braxton. The other was the shortest of the three with her long hair pulled back in a ponytail with a Delta baseball cap and she really did not look like she wanted to be at this party.

Mike grabbed James and pointed over in their direction, "Look man, why don't we go over and greet the ladies, because in the history of Houston Hall, I have never seen them at one of these parties". Mike and James walked over to the ladies and in unison said, "Hello ladies. My name is Mike and this is my boy James.

The ladies replied, "Hello".

The one with the big boobs, replied, "Hello my name is Gina Thomas, this is my friend Dez and the little one with the big attitude is Mikki".

"I don't have a big attitude Gina, but I really don't know why you dragged me to this party in the first place, I am too old to be partying with these youngsters!"

"Well ladies, please know that my boy mix master Chris is the deejay and this is his brother James and hope that you enjoy yourselves". With that being said, Gina grabbed Mike's arm and they hit the dance floor while Dez started dancing with James. Mikki decided to hang back and walked over to the deejay booth and just watched everything that was going on. After a couple of songs, Gina sauntered over to where Chris was spinning the records and started flirting with Chris. James came over and took a seat on the stage next to Mikki and they started talking. James did coax Mikki out on the dance floor but they kept getting interrupted by other females on the floor who wanted to talk to James or give him a hug.

Later that night Mikki and her friends said goodbye to James, Mike and Chris and started towards where they had parked their car. As they were walking to Mikki's car, they heard footsteps behind them and turned to see James and Mike walking behind them. Mike asked if they could walk with them because they had to walk to 39th street to get there car. Mikki was a little annoyed but told them that they were parked near 39th street as well.

As the 5 of them walked to the car, Gina flirted non-stop with both James and Mike. Mikki stayed quiet for the most part and answered yes or no questions, not willing to divulge too much information because she was just a little leery of these guys. When they got to 39th street they all realized that the guys were parked directly behind the girls. They continued to talk standing by the cars for a while and decided that since they still had two hours left on their meters that they would walk to Allegro pizza on 40th street and continue their conversation over pizza, Buffalo wings and beer. Once they got into the pizza place they all got a table and Mike and Gina continued to get cozier and exchanged numbers.

James decided that he was intrigued by Mikki but could not push up on her like that because she just was not turned on by sappy lines and fake charms. They all finished up their wings and walked back to their cars. They said good nite and James walked over to the driver side and asked Mikki if they could exchange numbers so that maybe they can hang out some time. Mikki gave James her phone number and told him that she would be relocating back to Philly in a couple of weeks so maybe if he called her then that they could possibly hook up.

James smiled, "Drive safe ladies".

Mike said, "Damn, James, you look sprung over that girl".

"Naw, man, just being a nice guy, some girls like nice guys."

A few weeks later, Mikki came home from her first day of orientation at her new job. She saw her parents sitting at the kitchen table drinking tea and said hello. That's when she saw a small bouquet of flowers.

"Daddy, you brought, mom some lilies, that's so nice, how was your day today?"

Her father looked up at her and smiled, "pumpkin now you know , I love your mother and all and I've loved her for 30 years but, I did not put out money for lilies when I can go in the back yard and clip roses from the our own bushes, and you know that your mother don't like lilies anyhow".

She smiled and kissed her mother on the forehead. "Well, whose flowers are they? Did Tim do something stupid again and send flowers to Leslie? "Girl, you know Tim don't have money like that to be spending on your sister especially with the both of them being in school and having the triplets!

"Well are you going to keep me in suspense any longer? Whose flowers are they?" Her parents replied in unison, "They're yours".

"Nice young man dropped them off for you earlier". Mikki's jaw dropped. "Mom, are you sure that Kevin did not just send someone with these flowers?" "No, they are not from Kevin, He said his name was James and he had on his Kappa Pin so you know I was impressed because you know your father is a Kappa. "Unlike Kevin, this young man, had manners and he asked if he could leave these for you because he knew that you had just moved back home".

Mikki stood with a look of awe on her father's face. "I don't know dad, Kevin may have done that to throw you off, and you know he tries to be slick like that".

Mikki's mother frowned when she walked back into the room. "I just hope that you are not fooled by that slick foolishness!"

"Mom, you know that Kevin and I are so over, especially after I found out that the girl named Tasha who was supposed to be his classmate is pregnant with his baby". "Well that is enough of talking about Kevin for one day; I'm going upstairs to call Gina and see what she is up to and maybe go out to dinner with her".

"Okay sweets", her parents said in unison.

Mikki went up to the room that she was currently sharing with her younger sister Monica who was not really happy about the situation and was a junior in high school. Mikki had to move back in with her parents because her apartment was not going to be ready until September 1st. It felt different for her to return to her parent's home after being in Pittsburgh for 3 years.

Mikki had completed her dual degree in Special Education and Elementary Education in 3 years instead of 4 and was glad that she was able to find a job working in special education after getting certified as a teacher after taking the Praxis. She felt proud of herself and she knew that her parents were as well. She flopped down on her bed and picked up the phone to call Gina. When she dialed Gina's phone number she got the answering machine and left Gina a message. As soon as she hung up the phone, the phone rang again and it was Gina.

"Hey girl, I was just calling to see if you wanted to go out for dinner and a movie". "Maybe we could head out to the $3 dollar movies in Yeadon and then go to Red Lobster in Springfield to have some shrimp".

"Gina, you know I just started working and I really do not have that much money saved up and I cannot be splurging on shrimp at Red Lobster".

"Who said you have to pay for your dinner or the movie for that matter?"

"What's that supposed to mean?"

"Well, it just means that I invited you and maybe I just want to celebrate that both of us graduating and are on our way to becoming successful in our careers".

"Gina, your butt is cheap and you never treated before, so who is this man and what have you done to him, in order for him to treat us to dinner?"

Gina laughed and said, "Girl you know me too well." "I have been in contact with the guy Mike that we met at the Black expo and he said that he didn't mind taking the both of us out to dinner, so we are kind of an item".

Mikki shook her head and laughed and said, "So which one of his boys are you two trying to hook me up with?"

Gina gasped, as if she was shocked and said, "Girl, you know, I would not try to pull a fast one on you. I know for a fact that you got some lilies today and you are perpetrating a fraud because you know that I know that those are your favorite flowers and that James dropped them off, so who do you think is also going to join us for dinner?"

Mikki sucked her teeth and then let out a long sigh. "Gina, you know that I am not ready for a relationship with anybody after what happened between Kevin and me!"

"Who said that it has to be a relationship, the boy sent you some flowers and wants to take you to a $3 movie in Yeadon and to a $9.99 all you can eat buffet, I hardly think it would hurt, especially since you are one broke sista right now!"

Mikki laughed, "Alright, as long as I can drive my own car because if the boy turns out to be psycho, I can drive myself home. Gina, what time does the movie start?" "Movie is at 8:10 and we will meet you there".

A little later that evening, Mikki poked her head into her parents room and let them know that she was going to hang out with Gina and some of their other friends and to say good night. She headed downstairs and grabbed a light sweater out of the hall closet and headed for her car which was parked across the street from her parent's house. She got into her car and headed to Yeadon for what she considered just a movie and dinner.

James paced nervously outside of his car which was parked in the back of the Yeadon movie theater. He knew that he was a little bold when he left the flowers at Mikki's house, but when he first met her; he really felt a good vibe about her. He was waiting for Gina and Mike to pull up; those two had been hot and heavy ever since they met. He laughed; "I know that I cannot definitely push up on Mikki like Mike did with Gina". He spotted Mike pull up with Gina in her Volkswagen Jetta and smiled, he could at least calm down a bit, his boy was there to back him up. Mike and Gina walked towards him holding hands and giggling, he just shook his head, and thought, they both got their nose wide open for each other.

"Hey, James", Gina, said. "Wassup frat, Mike said. James walked over to Gina and gave her a hug and gave Mike a hand shake. James looked at Gina and said, "Well, is she going to join us?"

Gina shook her head and said, "Yes James she decided to join us".

"Good, I really did not want to be the third wheel with you to pawing all over each other".

Gina sucked her teeth and slapped James on the shoulder. "Here she comes now, lover boy. James stared at Gina and they all walked over to where Mikki had parked her car. She got out and hugged Gina and said hello to Mike and James. They all went to catch the movie. After the movie and having to listen to Gina and Mike slobber all over each other, they all headed up to the Red Lobster. Once in Red Lobster, they all sat down and ordered their drinks and meals.

"So, Mikki, what do you think of my boy?"

Gina slapped Mike on the shoulder, "why you sweating my girl like that? If she like your boy, she will let him know!"

"Well, if she does like my boy, she betta let him know, 'cause, he has a whole stable of females trying to mack him!"

Mikki frowned and looked over at Mike, "so I guess that means that you have a whole stable of females trying to mack you too?"

" Naw, I'm just trying to be with your girl Gina, that's why when we exchanged numbers, I definitely broke the don't call the next day rule with her and I called her the next morning to see if she wanted to do breakfast."

"Gina, you broke the rules of the chase by going out with him the very next day?"

"Shoot girl, he was fine and I was trying to spend some time, if you know what I mean!"

Mikki turned to James who just sat and watched everything going on. "And what do you have to say about all of this Mr. Stevens?

"Leave me and the mack game out of this! I just thought that we had nice conversation when we met, and I wanted to at least hang out with you again, for the possibility of being friends, because I am just not ready to mack any females who may be in my stable because, I need to work on my career and make sure that my family is taken care of."

"Your family, what do you have children?"

"No, I am the oldest son in my family, I was raised by mother and I have 3 siblings."

"Oh, that is very nice of you."

The rest of the evening went on with just playful banter and they all parted their ways.

When Gina got home her sisters Monica and Jamie were watching TV in the living room. "Hey guys, wassup?

"Nothing they both answered, they were watching videos on BET.

"Mikki, you have a message by the answering machine in the kitchen, Kevin called", Jamie said.

"Did you take the message?"

"No, I think mom did, and she did not seem happy that he called".

"Okay, I'll get it in the morning; I am tutoring at the school with dad so I need to be well rested".

The next morning while she was having some tea, she decided that she would call Kevin and find out why he was still calling. She dialed his number and a woman answered on the second ring. "Good morning, may I speak with Kevin?"

"Sure may I tell him whose calling?"

"Yes, could you please tell him that it is Mikki?"

Whoever the woman was she sucked her teeth and handed the phone to Kevin after telling him that is was Mikki.

"Hello?"

"Hello Kevin, it's Mikki, I was just returning your call from yesterday". "I was out when you called and left the message with my mother".

Hey baby, how are you?" Kevin went into smooth talking mode, "I just called to see how you were doing, how the new job was coming, make sure you were alright".

"Kevin, let's not go there, we agreed to be friends, and the hey baby act is dead". "You forget that you have a baby on the way and the female you should be sweet talking is the one that is carrying your baby".

"Hey, Hey Mikki let's not be so defensive, I called you because, Tasha and I wanted to ask you if you would be the godmother of our child". "We know that it is a girl and we decided that we wanted to name her Kayla Arielle Lewis, so she will have the same initials as her daddy".

Mikki rolled her eyes and took a deep breath before she spoke. "Kevin, I really do not think that my being the god-mother to your baby would be a good idea, I mean, Tasha and I really have no relationship what so ever, and I told you more than a dozen times that I am not trying to see you like that, we have been so over for months now". "Since you told me that Tasha was expecting your baby"

"Mikki, I really do not see it that way, you and I may not be a couple anymore, but I always respected you as a good friend of mine". "We have history to back in the days when we used to play hide go seek and catch a girl get a girl on 18th street".

"Yeah well, those were our grade school years and I definitely know that we are not living in those times anymore".

"Mikki, please do this for me? You know that Tasha is not from Philly and she does not have any family here, and I just want her to have some type of stability for her sake and for the baby's sake".

"Look, I will think about it and I will get back to you in about a week or two". Mikki hung up the phone and thought about calling Gina to talk to her but knew that Gina was working a 12 hour shift at the hospital. Mikki decided to call her good friend Michele and catch up with her and see how life was treating her at school.

Michele and Mikki were friends since they were 8 and 6 years old. Although Michele was younger, she and Mikki lived next door to each other and Michele always was wise beyond her years. She graduated high school at 16 with Mikki and headed right to Howard to major in Pre-Med. Michele was in her 1st year of Medical School, because she too like Mikki had finished her getting her bachelor degree in 3 years.

Mikki picked up the phone and dialed Michele. "Hey, Michele, what's going on girl?"

"Nothing much, a little tired from this first week of Med school at Penn but, I will make it".

"Girl, I just got off the phone with Kevin and he asked me to be the godmother to his baby with Tasha".

"You're kidding me right?"

" No, I definitely heard him right, and he tried to play it like, well since we are no longer a couple, we can still be friends and Tasha has no family here in Philly and I just want her to have a support system when she has this baby".

"Mikki, I know that the break up was nasty between you and Kevin, because of the slimy tactics he was pulling while you were in Pittsburgh, being loyal- but what do I always tell you about forgiveness?"

"Look, I know what you say about forgiveness, I'm starting to think you got it from Oprah!" "I'll think about it, but I am not going to give him a quick answer".

"Well how about, I change the subject, how nice is this guy that is jocking you? "

"James is nice, but I am definitely trying to take it slow with him. I really do not think that I am ready to have a steady just yet".

"Well, girl I do have to go, my studies are calling me". "How about we go to jazz brunch at Zanzibar tomorrow?" "Call Gina and see if she can drag her butt away from Mike and we can just do us girls!"

"Alright, I will and I am sure since food is involved, she will come". Mikki looked over and saw that the answering machine light was blinking so she pushed the button and listened to the messages.

"Beep- Hey ma, this is Leslie, I wanted to know if you could watch the triplets for me after church tomorrow, I have a study group at 2pm and I don't have anyone to watch them for me." "Call me".

"Beep- This message is for Mikki, uh this is James and I wanted to just say thank you for hanging out with me the tonight. I hope that we can hang out again sometime. I know you have my number". "Talk to you soon".

Mikki smiled. James was a nice guy she thought but she was not going to rush into anything to soon with him.

Mikki

Mikki stretched out in bed and realized that James was not there to spoon with her and it was all her doing. She played back what her mother and Aunt Marcy had said to her when she told them how fast she went to court and filed separation papers. Her mother said that she was being too harsh, but Mikki really believed that James needed to realize that his mother was interfering with their lives and it needed to stop. Mikki rubbed her head and felt the onset of a major headache; she was having a lot of them lately. She sat up and reached over and turned on the light on her nightstand and just began to cry. She never in a million years thought that the man of her dreams would make her play second fiddle to another woman. Especially when the woman was his mother.

Mikki wiped her eyes and heard the pitter patter of little feet coming down the hall. She knew that she had to get herself together because that was Jason, Skyler and Shannon coming down the hall to get in bed with her. Ever since James moved out the twins and Jason came down the hall faithfully at about 4 in the morning and cuddled with her until they started their day. The door swung open and she saw Skyler first with Jason and Shannon bringing up the rear. She smiled, if anything, the kids would be her saving grace and help her through this tough time without James being at home.

"Alright, climb in you three, and make sure that you guys go to the bathroom so that we do not have any accidents".

The three of them shook their heads in unison and all walked down the hall to her master bathroom and waited quietly in line to have their turn at going before they climb into Mikki's bed. A lot of people when they saw those three together believed that they were triplets because Jason, although at age 3 was 16 months younger than the girls, was just as tall as they were and the girls were very protective of him as well. They all settled in and Mikki turned off the light so that they could get some rest.

James

James had tossed and turned all night long. He knew that he had to be at the house in the morning so that he could go to church with Mikki and the kids. He hated that although they were separated, he still wanted to make sure that he participated in all of the important times in their children's lives. He looked over at the clock and saw that he had 3 hours before he was to even get up. He pulled the covers back over his head and thought, tried to go back to sleep. Just then the phone rang.

James rolled over and picked up the phone, "Hello?"

"Good morning son, how are you this morning?"

"Mom, do you know what time it is?"

"Yes son, its 6:15 and I have to be to work". "Don't you remember, I left a message on your machine and said that I have to be to work at 7 and I need a ride"?

"No, I did not listen to my messages when I got home because I was tired from spending time with the boys".

"Oh, well, how soon can you get here?" "I just can't be late for work you know".

"I'll be there in 10, but please be ready".

James hung up the phone and grabbed his sweats from the side of the bed and put them on. He picked up his car keys and slid on his Nike slides and headed out his apartment. On his way out of the apartment building he spoke to his neighbor Frank. James continued to his truck and looked at the bumper sticker that his oldest son Steven insisted that he put somewhere in his truck. My child is an honor roll student at Strath Haven Elementary. He smiled and jumped in so that he could make sure that his mother Regina could get to work.

He didn't get it, His mother could take the bus to work, but for some reason he was always the one to drive her. Her husband Russell did not drive at all so whenever, his mother wanted to go somewhere and she felt that she wanted to be chauffeured around she called him. He was just being a good son to his mother, but Mikki just could not get it through her head. James was tired, he could not deal with the situation his life had turned out to be. He loved his wife, he missed his family and he decided that he would do whatever Mikki wanted him to do, so that he could be back at his home in the suburbs and not some studio apartment in the city.

James pulled up in front of his mother's house and honked the horn. The door opened and his sister Rita opened the door and told him that his mom would be right out. He loved his sister Rita but she was the epitome of hoochie round the way girl.

She was 28 and had two little girls by the same guy. She partied to all hours of the night, she did not go to college like James and she still lived at home with his mom and her father Russell and although she had once lived in her own apartment, she had just recently returned and James did not see her ever moving out.

His mom came down the steps with all of her bags and James stepped out of the car to help her. At age 54, James' mother Regina looked much older and she carried herself that way as well.

"Hey, mom let me get that for you". "Thanks son".

"Yes, because we need to get a move on if you are going to get to work on time".

They both climbed in the car and took off.

"James, how are the kids doing?"

"They are fine mom, after I drop you off, I need to go and get a shower so that I can make sure that I go to church with them".

"So does Mikki go along or is going to church one of her rules for when and how you can spend time with your kids?" "How can she get away with this son?" "She puts you out of your own house, and you have to abide by her rules on when you can spend time with your children?" "Maybe you are better of not being married to that conniving little winch!"

James frowned, "Mom, I know you are concerned for me, but we always go to church together and Mikki is by no means manipulating anything, I have full access to the children, there are no rules set that I can't see the children at any time".

"Well, is she seeing someone else? I can't understand why you have to be separated if nothing is going on with your marriage. I just bet she's seeing someone else?"

James slapped his hand on the dash board. "Mom- Mikki and I were having problems and just leave it at that!" "It is none of your business why we are separated and just leave it be! "Mikki and I will work this thing out! Just leave it be!"

"Humph! I was just concerned about you being able to see your children, if you and little Miss Bourgeois don't get back together, I really don't care". "I just want to make sure she doesn't keep your children and my grandchildren from the family!"

"Mom, are you out of your mind! You don't spend that much time with the kids anyway, you're too busy playing mommy to Rita's kids and you still have two teenage sons who sit around and do nothing!"

"I did not spend that much time with your children because of your wife and her special terms for your children! Maybe it's better that you do have visitation rights, maybe you can bring the children here to spend more time with your side of the family and not wind up as bourgeois as their mother".

"Damn it mom, you will not continue to talk about my wife like that! I will not listen to you and I will cut all ties from you all together". "Mikki is still my wife and you will not disrespect her to me or to my children!"

"Alright, James, I will not say anything else to you but, I think you need to realize that you got in way over your head when you decided that you were going to marry miss-goody two shoe wife of yours".

For the rest of the ride to his mom's job at Pennsylvania Hospital, they said nothing. James was furious. Since he moved into his apartment, he felt that his mother was demanding more of his time than ever. In the past week alone, he had taken her to Target twice, BJ's wholesale club, Queen Village to pick up meat, he took her to 3 different supermarkets because of sales, Kmart, Sears, and Wal-Mart and to the new Lowe's superstore on Delaware Avenue. James was concerned that maybe he was going to burn out from all of the driving and spending time with mother and her family in general.

Mikki

"Steven! Will you please bring me your shirt so that it can be ironed?" "You know that we need to get ready for church". "Your dad will be here in about ½ an hour and he said that after church we can go out to breakfast".

"Ooh! I know what I want for breakfast, I want stuffed crepes with Strawberries and whipped cream cheese", shouted Skyler and Shannon.

"I want pancakes, shouted Jason!"

"I don't want to go to breakfast; I just want my daddy to be back at home with us!" Scott sulked.

Mikki ran over to Scott and gave him a hug, "I know Scott, mommy and daddy are trying to work things out so that daddy can be back at home and we will try and get it done as soon as possible".

Mikki wanted to cry, but she knew that she could not cry in front of the children. Mikki knew that she had to take a stand with James but did she go too far? She still loved James, but was she willing for the kid's sake to welcome him back home and forget the separation?

Just then, she heard the garage door open and knew that it was James pulling in.

"Kids, I think that is your daddy, so why don't you go downstairs and talk to daddy while mommy finishes getting dressed so that we can get to church on time".

"Daddy!" The kids screamed as they ran downstairs.

Mikki took a little more time than usual getting ready for church. Her 5'2" frame was petite but she had curves. Having 5 children did not seem to have left extra fluff. Mikki made sure that her shoulder length hair was in place. She grabbed her purse and the baby bag off the bench in front of her bed and went downstairs to hear the children in the family room detailing to James all that happened this week.

James looked up to see Mikki come down the steps and smiled. Mikki always looked good to him, but he had not seen much of her since the separation because he was spending so much time with the kids or at his mother's house. Mikki had good taste; she had on a pink polka dot dress with pink and black pumps. The dress was an a-line dress that showed off her curves, it had an empire waste and it was really flowy at the bottom. She carried a black and pink canvas coach bag that doubled as a children activity bag in which she carried snacks for the kids while they were in children's church as well as sippy cups for Jason and the twins, Steven and Scotts' game boys and extra games and coloring books and crayons for all.

"Well, I'm ready", James said.

"And hello and good morning to you James", Mikki replied.

"I'm sorry, good morning Mikki", and he walked over and gave her a kiss on the cheek.

"James, could you please tell your children that we are going to breakfast after church and that you will be staying here all day?"

"Yes children, your mother is right, we planned to have a whole day full of fun".

"Well, let's get a move on guys".

James looked at Mikki and whispered thank you as they all walked out to the garage. Mikki opened the doors on her Mercedes ML350 to get the car seats out and put them into James' Sequoia. James let Steven and Scott get into the third row seat and then started to load the little ones' car seats in and loaded them in one by one. After everyone was loaded in, they headed for church.

After church was over, they all decided that they would go to IHOP because the kids all had different ideas on what they wanted to eat for breakfast.

"James, I wanted to talk to you about working on you coming back home", Mikki said. James looked at Mikki in awe. This is what he wanted to talk to her about.

"You must have read my mind, James answered.

"I have been thinking about it really hard lately and I know that it has just been a little over a month, the children made me realize that they need you, I want you to come back home, but I want you to understand that we need to go to counseling and work on our relationship". "I think that we should go to counseling so that maybe someone else can give you an idea of what I am talking about with your mom".

"Mikki, you know that I love you more than anything in the world and when I got served with those papers, I really could not deal, I know that I had to be strong for the children, but I could not deal". "You are my best friend, and I will do whatever it takes to make this work between us".

"Okay, then for now it's settled, you can move back home, but I want you to sleep in the guest room for now until we get some things worked out".

"That's fine; I will do whatever, so that I can be back home with you guys as a family".

Just then, James cell phone rang. "Hello, yeah, hey mom, I need to call you back because, Mikki and the children and I are at breakfast". "I will call you later". James closed his cell phone and looked Mikki in her eyes.

"I will make this work for us babe, I promise".

"I hope so, Mikki said. "I really hope so".

James and Mikki looked up as the waitress brought their food to the table. Let's say grace kids. They all bowed their heads and Skylar, Jason and Shannon all said in unison, "Great food, big feet, good god let's eat!" Steven and Scott laughed and they all began to eat. After finishing their meal they packed up their children and went home.

Mikki, Gina and Michele all walked into Zanzibar blue and it was packed. "Looks, like we won't be getting served at the jazz brunch today", Gina sighed.

"Hey why don't we go to Fridays on South Street, we should be able to get a table especially because everybody and their damn mother looks like they are here instead!"

"Sounds like a plan to me, what do you think Michele?"

"Yes, my stomach is talking to me and I do not want to be waiting 2 hours to sip some mimosas and have a nice meal". They walked out of Zanzibar blue and headed on Broad Street towards South Street. Gina had parked her Toyota corolla at a meter near there and they could just head down South Street. They got in the car drove down South Street to 4th made a right turn and immediately found parking. Once they parked the car they headed back onto South Street and walked 2 blocks down and went to Friday's. When they got to Fridays, they only had a 10 minute wait so they decided to go and sit at the bar while they waited.

"Michele, so how does it feel to officially be a Med student?" Gina asked.

"Girl, it is hectic, there is a lot of studying, but I can say one thing, there are a lot of cute guys in my classes, but I can tell if they are marriage material if they make it through the first year".

"Girl, you know that you never change, you have been looking for the perfect husband since, we went to Tameka's sweet sixteen party and that was years ago".

"Girl, I have a plan going, I need to be married with the right husband by the time I am 25. "I want to be trying to push out babies by the time I am 28 and done by the time I am 32". "Especially if I space them to be at least 18 months apart". "I want 2 children that's all".

Mikki shook her head and laughed, "Girl you cannot plan everything in your life, you have to just let it flow". "And how do you know that, your mister right is going to come and agree with all you have planned?"

" Let's see, I am 20 now , I am in my first year of medical school, as long as I graduate on time, I will be 24 and passing the boards and beginning my residency so that gives me some time to find mister right instead of mister right now like our girl Gina over here!"

"Girl, let me tell you something, Mike is mister right now and could possibly become mister long term for me". "Mike is so sweet, caring and he gets me". "Mike is a special kind of man if he really gets you!"

The server came over and let the ladies know that their table was ready. They headed to the table when Mikki noticed that two guys were motioning in their direction.

"Gina, do you know those guys over there?"

Gina turned around, "yes I think that is Mike's friend James who went to the movies with us when we went to Yeadon but I do not know the other guy that he was with".

Gina grabbed Mikki's hand, "come on, let's go over and say hello".

"No, I don't want to bother him and a real lady lets a man come over and speak to them".

"Well, I'm just an around the way girl and we go and say hello to people that we know!" Gina grabbed her hand and they walked over to where James was sitting with his friend.

"Hi, James, how are you, Gina asked?"

"Hi Gina, Hello Mikki, how are you?"

"We're fine and who is this gentleman sitting with you?"

"Mikki, Gina this is my friend Zavier, we go way back to grade school". "We went to Zanzibar for brunch but it was too crowded so we decided to come here instead".

"Well we better get back to our friend Michele so that she won't get lonely".

"Well hey, we haven't ordered yet, why don't we see if they can seat us together if you don't mind?"

"Sure, I will grab Michele and see if we can make it happen".

The server pushed the table next to James and his friend Zavier and they all sat together. James introduced himself and Zavier to Michele and they all got comfy. They were laughing and carrying on when who did they see walk into the restaurant but Mikki's ex Kevin, his mother and Tasha the girl that he impregnated.

Mikki felt like she wanted to shrink down in her chair. Wasn't it just days ago that she had spoke to him on the phone about being the god mother to his unborn child. Kevin's mother saw her first and waved hello at Mikki. Mikki excused herself from the table and walked to where they were seated.

"Hello, Mrs. Lewis, how are you?"

"Well Mikki, it is nice to see you again, how is everything going with your new job?"

"Teaching is a new experience for me". "It is different from student teaching, but I will get the hang of it eventually".

"I'm so glad for you".

"Hello Kevin and Tasha", Mikki said.

Tasha waved hello and tried to play demure as Kevin's mother looked on.

"Well, Mikki it was good to see you again, and tell your parents that I said hello".

As Mikki began to walk away, Tasha asked if she had made a decision on whether or not she was going to be the godmother of her baby. Mikki let her know that she would give her an answer before the end of the following week. Tasha said thanks and sat back down next to Kevin.

When Mikki got back to the table with her friends, Michele tugged her on the arm and asked her if that was the famous Tasha. "In the flesh", Mikki answered.

James asked, "What was that all about".

"Well to make a long story short", Gina interrupted, "the guy is Mikki's ex-boyfriend that she played little miss faithful to for the last 2 years of college and the girl is who was supposed to be only a classmate that ended up pregnant by him that they are now asking Mikki to be the godmother to".

Mikki just put her head in her face and shook her head.

"I'm sorry and I am not trying to be in your business, but no good man would try and put the both of you women thru such an ordeal", said Zavier.

"I say amen to that", chimed in Michele.

"I also say good riddance to bad rubbish, because any man who has someone being faithful to him from afar and he still getting over and hooking up with other woman is not worth the time of day!" "And I guess that is why he's never crossed to become a kappa!"

They all laughed and finished their desert and split the tab so that they could go their separate ways. On the way out, Zavier asked to speak to Michele alone while Gina, Mikki and James waited.

"It was nice seeing you again Mikki, you know that you are good company, and I hope that seeing your ex did not spoil your fun", said James.

"No, I am over him, but I still seethe when I think that he cheated on me with her and now he has the audacity to ask me to be the god-mother of their child".

"Well, you have to give it to him on some level, he is trying to kick game, but I know a strong woman like you is not going to concede to him and let him win".

"Thanks, James, I did have a nice time hanging with you and your friend, I hope that we can hang out again".

"Me, too Mikki, Me too".

Zavier and Michele came walking back to where James, Mikki and Gina were standing and said their last goodbyes and walked away in opposite directions. As the ladies walked back to their cars, Mikki and Gina chided Michele about Zavier and how he could possibly fit into her plan of med school and having a baby by age 28.

"Well, I have to tell you ladies, He was 6'4, Has nice brown eyes, dark wavy hair and his complexion is the color of mocha". "He could fit in very nicely especially because he is getting his master's degree in public health administration, so that means, I can be the doctor and he can run my hospital!"

The three of them laughed and rounded the corner on 4th street to go back to Gina's car and head home.

"James, please tell me that you are definitely trying to hook up with that girl Mikki? Zavier asked as they walked to their cars.

"I do like her but, she has been spurned by that guy Kevin that she went over to talk to when we were in Fridays".

"Oh, I see, but man, have you taken her out on a date besides just being amongst friends like today?"

"No, the last time we went out we were out with Mike and her friend Gina".

"Don't you think you at least owe it to yourself to ask her out on one date to see if she is feeling you as much as you are feeling her?"

"No doubt, but I think that it should wait awhile because I have some things going on at home".

"Man, don't tell me it's your moms again?"

"No not specifically, you know that my sister Rita is pregnant and she is only 16 and my mom's is definitely not happy about it".

"Well, your step-dad is there, why can't he handle what's going on?"

" He's involved, but you know this has become a family issue because, my moms is trying to stress to Rita that she needs to graduate high school and go to college like I did, but Rita is not hearing any of that".

Zavier frowned, "yo man, I know you want to be there for your family, but just remember you have your life to live also and handling Rita should be something that your moms and your step – dad should handle".

"I understand where you're coming from Z but family is family". They continued up Lombard Street to 5th where they had parked their cars.

"Yo man, I'll try to hook up with you later on this week and I hope that you think about what I said with this Mikki girl, if you are really feeling her you better let her know".

"I know man, I'll think about it". James got in his car and turned on his radio to listen to Smooth Jazz 106.1 to calm his nerves. I really do not want to try and be in a relationship right now. *Especially after all of the drama with Tammy, but I really like this girl Mikki and its funny how we just keep running into each other*, James thought to himself. *I'm going to just chill and if it happens that we* hang *out again, I will just go with the flow*. When James got to his apartment, he saw that he had messages on his machine.

"Beep- Hey James this is your big sister, Janice, I wanted to remind you that the rehearsal dinner for my wedding is next Friday at 6pm at my church on Federal Street in south Philly. The address is 1836-40 Federal Street and the name of the church is Solid Rock Baptist Church". "And please be on time, we only can be in the church for 2 hours and I really do not want to wait for anyone".

"Beep- James this is your mother, I need you to call me as soon as you get this message- thanks.

"Beep-yo frat, it's Mike, I wanted to give you a buzz to see what you are trying to get into tonight, Gina and I are trying to catch a movie, so let me know".

"Beep- James this is your mother again- Please call me".

"Beep- James this is your brother Chris, I just wanted to remind you that I need your help moving my deejay equipment to the storage facility while we paint our house, give me call when you get a chance".

After playing all of the messages, James called his brother Chris back and let him know that he would be there later in the day to help him move his equipment. Chris was his half brother on his father's side and it was funny because he and Chris were only 11 months apart. He then called his half sister Janice and let her know that he did not forget that her wedding rehearsal was next Friday and he would be on time for that as well, because he would be coming straight from work. Janice was older than him by 21 months. James laughed to himself and thought that his father Jackson had been a very busy man. His father had 6 children by 3 different women and his second wife who already had 3 children was pregnant with the 4th.

I know that I really will not have to worry about any major gaps in the ages of my children because I do not plan on having any children out of wedlock or be forced to get married young like my dad was forced to when he married Janice and Chris's mother. Although, James mother never married his father, James was grateful that he only spent time with his father when needed because his father was a bonafide knuckle head.

James picked up the phone and called his mother, to see what she was so important. "Hello, Hey mom wassup?"

"I called you because I wanted to go to Target this afternoon, because I need to get school supplies for Rita, Jordan and little Russell".

"Mom, I really have some things that I need to get done, can I take you another time?"

"James, we discussed this, my time is limited due to my work schedule and I need to get these things done, so that everyone is ready for school when it starts in a couple of weeks".

"Mom, I understand that but you don't live to far from CVS and the new dollar store on Oregon Avenue, can't you send Rita down there?"

"James, you know that I cannot count on her with my money, I would rather do it myself".

James bit down on his lip, so that he would not get into it with his mother, James could not understand why at age 16 Rita could not just go and buy the things that his mom wanted to go and pick up. When he was 16 he was working and he was responsible for the house, and babysitting Rita, Jordan and Russell with no problems. He thought to himself, that his mother let Rita get away with too much.

"Mom, I can take you but you have to be ready in the next half hour because, I have to help Chris move his equipment and I plan on going to the movies later with some friends".

"Okay, son, I'll see you when you get here". James sped to his mother's house so that he could take her shopping and get her errands done and over with. When he walked in, he saw his two brothers, little Russell and Jordan playing Sega on the big screen in the living room while their father Russell, Sr. was fast asleep on the couch.

"Hey wassup you two?" Neither one of them opened their mouths to say hello in return. Just then his sister Rita came down the steps looking more than 4 months pregnant.

"Eww! Look what the cat drug in", Rita said pointing at her brother.

"I know you are not one to talk about anybody, especially because you look like someone put a basketball under your shirt and you are about to tip over!" James retaliated.

"Ha-ha! That's what I tell her all the time", Jordan laughed.

"Ma! Come on! I told you that I have some other things to do".

"I thought you said that you were going to go and help Chris first?"

"No, I did not, Chris is at work, so I came to get you first and I need to meet him by six to move his equipment".

"Okay, give me five minutes, and I will be down, I need to put some clothes on"

. James rolled his eyes and sat on the love seat behind where his brothers were sitting on the floor.

"Rita, are they going to let you go to school until you have the baby?"

"I can go to Southern until I am 7 months along and then I have to go to a school for pregnant teenagers until the baby is 2 months old and then I can return to my regular classes".

"So do you know who the baby's father is?"

"Yes, I do, it's the guy that I have been dating for the last year, Sean".

"What Sean are you talking about?" "Sean that lives on 22nd street?"

"Yes, that Sean".

"Girl, are you out of your mind? Sean has 4 children already that he does not take care of!"

Rita sighed.

"What do think that because you're Rita, he's going to make special arrangements to be a daddy to yours?" "I know the whole family, his brother and I graduated the same year". "What does mom have to say about this?"

Rita shrugged her shoulders and lowered her head.

Little Russell looked up from his game and said, "That's who she was cutting school with, when daddy caught them here!"

"Shut up Russell, I told you to mind your business!"

"And what did Russell say?"

"He didn't say anything, he just took me to the health center and made sure that I got condoms and told me to be careful".

James balled up his fist and shook Russell. "Russell, you mean to tell me that you caught her cutting school and all you could do was take her to get condoms?"

"James, don't tell me how to raise my child in my house, she's my damn daughter and you ain't nobody but her high faluting know it all brother!" "Ran off to college to shirk your responsibilities at home!" "Man, I ought to punch you lights out!" "Who do you think you are, that's my damn child and I do right by her every day!" "So stay out of this!"

"Ma! Do you hear this nonsense your husband is talking?" "That's why your daughter is pregnant today- your husband did his fatherly duties and took her to get condoms!" "I'm outta here, let your lazy husband do his fatherly duties and take you to get school supplies for his own children, I can't take this!"

Regina ran after her son and tried to calm him down but to no avail, James just got in his car and took off.

Mikki was delighted that tomorrow her apartment would be ready to move in. She loved her family, but having to live in such close quarters with her younger sisters and two brothers and her parents was starting to drive her crazy. She had already packed most of her stuff and she did not have to worry about the bed that she currently slept in, because it was already there when she came back home. She had it all set, in the morning she would go and pick up the keys from the rental office and then head to work. After work she would go to her parent's house and meet Michele, Gina and Dez at her parents and they would move her stuff so that she could get settled in her new apartment. It would feel so good. Her phone was set to be turned on first thing Tuesday morning and it would be so good to not have to listen to Jamie and Monica argue over which boys liked them at school or in the neighborhood. She would not have to listen to her little brothers Mark and Joey argue over Sega games, or who was better at gymnastics and football or Power ranger cartoons. It would be her first slice of heaven since she had been home. The phone rang and Mikki reached over to grab the phone before her cackling sisters did.

"Hello? Hello, May I speak with Mikki please?"

"Yes this is, may I ask who is calling?"

"It's James. Oh, hello James, how are you?"

"I doing fine, I just wanted to give you a call to see if you enjoyed yourself this afternoon, because, I certainly did enjoy you and your friend's company."

"It was nice; I really had my mind set on getting some sweet potato fries from Zanzibar. But I did eat a lot when we were at Fridays".

"Well, maybe next time, I can take you to Zanzibar for dinner, how about that?"

That does sound nice, but James, I need to remind you that I really just want to be friends".

"Mikki, I know, after your break up with Kevin it is going to be hard and that is all that I can offer you as well at this time". "Just friends, hanging out, doing dinner sometimes and just hanging out".

"I can accept that James, so friend, what's going on with you?"

"Nothing much, I am just trying to get myself ready for work tomorrow and I just got back from helping my brother Chris take his equipment and put it in storage". "He will not be doing any parties for the next three weeks and his wife Charmaine does not like him to keep it in the house, because their house is so small".

"That's good that you help your siblings out. But, living here with my younger siblings is going to drive me crazy that is why I cannot wait until I have the keys to my apartment tomorrow and move in".

"Oh, I see someone is moving up in the world? Where are you moving to? I am moving to Parkview Court apartments in Yeadon".

"Oh, I know where that is, I actually live in University City near Penn on Hazel Avenue. I have a one bedroom apartment, which is pretty nice".

"Mikki, would you like to go and get some ice cream with me? I was in the mood and friends do that sort of thing right?"

"Sure James, how about I meet you at the Baskin Robbins on 40th street. I need to throw on some sweats and I will meet you there".

"Sure that's cool, I'll see you in about 30 minutes".

"Sure see you soon". Mikki hung up the phone and change into her red sweatpants with her sorority insignia stitched on the knee and her Duquesne University women's basketball sweatshirt. She pulled her hair back into a ponytail and grabbed her car keys off the dresser and headed out. When she got downstairs, she saw that her mother was sitting in the living room drinking tea and watching the news.

"Hey mom, I'm going to head out to Baskin Robbins for ice cream". "Don't wait up".

Her mom smiled, "girl you know that it is already past my bedtime, I just sat down to watch the news, I'm headed up".

"Okay well, I'll see you later". Mikki got into her car and decided that she would take the scenic route to Baskin Robbins. She made a left onto Federal Street and followed it until she got to 24th street, made a left and followed 24th street to Oakford and followed Oakford Street to 30th so that she could go over the Grays Ferry Bridge. Once she got to 40th and walnut, she was lucky to find a parking space a few doors down from Baskin Robbins. She parked her car and put the club on and headed over to Baskin Robbins. Once she crossed the street and got directly in front of Baskin Robbins she saw James coming from the other direction because he had parked on the other side of 40th street.

"Hey Mikki, I see we both made perfect timing, so how about that ice cream?"

"Sure".

Mikki

It had been a week since James had come back home and things were going okay. Mikki had let James know that when she asked him to come back home, they would have to work at being a family again, and he would have to listen to what she was saying to him. The test of if he had been listening was coming up for the next weekend; She and James had made plans to take the children to the Garden State Discovery Museum over in Cherry Hill and then to the Chinese Buffet afterwards first thing in the morning on Saturday. Mikki knew that Regina had to work 3pm – 11pm on Friday, so she would need to have to arrange for a ride home so that James would not have to make the trek from their house in Wallingford, into center city Philadelphia to pick her up. Mikki was waiting on pins and needles to what would happen.

Just then, James came into their kitchen and kissed her on the cheek. "Hey babe, what are you planning in that great mind of yours?"

"Nothing, I was just thinking about our upcoming plans for the kids this weekend". "Scott and Steven have been begging to bring friends along, because they claim that they will not have fun with Skylar, Shannon and Jason because they are younger". "I told them I would think about it and let them know in enough time to make arrangements with their friends' parents if I decide to allow them to bring friends".

"Well, if they bring friends that means that we are going to have to drive both cars, my car only seats 8 and with the 2 booster seats for the girls and the car seat for Jason there is no additional room for 2 more people".

"Well, it's not a definite, I am still thinking about it for now- it's only Sunday".

The phone rings and Mikki grabs it from the base.

"Hello, Hey Gina, how are you, long time no hear!" "Congratulations, sweetie, I am so happy for you!" "James, Gina says hello and her and Mike are expecting again!"

"Tell them both that I said congratulations". Honey, I will be back, I am going to take Steven and Scott to play hoops at Rainbow playground". "The girls and Jason are napping so we will be back in about 2 hours in enough time for dinner".

"Okay, see you hon!" Mikki could now devote time to talking candidly to Gina on the phone.

"So Mikki, how has it been going since you let James come back home?" "Any interference from his mother?"

" No, not so far, but it has only been a week and you know the slick one is just trying to lay low, so she can attack the jugular at will". "Anyway, so I will be having another god child in about 7 months!" I am so happy for you and Mike, but I miss you guys, especially because you guys are in North Carolina, and we only get to see you if we drive down for a visit or if you guys happen to be here for a family function". "There is too much distance between us girl and I miss you!"

"I miss you to Mikki, but I am also calling with more good news". "Mike is being relocated to Maryland, so I will be closer to you because we are looking for homes in Owings Mills". "We will be going to look at some houses on Saturday and we can come to visit you guys on Sunday and we can go to church and have brunch".

"Oh, girl, I am so excited that you guys will be closer, Michele just bought a house in Aston, so we will definitely be seeing more of each other".

"Now Mikki, let's get back to the James situation, do you really believe that allowing him back into the house so soon will make your situation change?"

"No, but I can try, Gina, you know that I love my husband, but I refuse to let him kill his self trying to take care of two households". "His mother is married and has been married for years, her husband does nothing, if something breaks in the house, she calls James, and if Jordan or little Russell gets out of line or into trouble she calls James". "If she wants to borrow money, she calls James". "It's ridiculous, James is her child and she should not depend on him like that".

"Sometimes, I feel like I am the second wife and she is the angry first wife who is making him pay because he got a younger model!"

"Girl you are crazy, but I understand what you are saying. She wants to be his first priority, but she is his mother and you are his wife and you should definitely come first".

"So enough about me Gina, How is my god son MJ, doing? Well you know MJ is MJ, he is so used to being the only child, and he has not come to grips with the fact that there will be a baby in this house. Just think about it, MJ will be 13 this year and it will be a little hard for me to have the two extremes a baby and a 13 year old know it all".

"Girl it seems to me that you are going to have your hands full! Do you know if you are going to have a boy or a girl?"

"We decided to wait until we have the baby and find out the sex". "Well, I love you, I miss you and I can't wait to see you on Sunday, girl". "I need to go and lie down and take a nap before my three little ones wake up and unleash havoc on this house". "Call me later in the week and I will let you know if I can get Michele over here for Sunday brunch".

"Mikki, what about Tasha, how is she doing?"

"Tasha is fine, she was here last night with Kayla who is 13 now and she is so tall".

"Oh my gosh, is Kayla that old?"

"Yes girl, Tasha has her hands full especially because Kyle is 4 and Kirby is 2 and they are expecting another one, I believe that Tasha is due in about 4 months".

"Oh wow, her and Kevin have been really busy?"

"Yes, not to mention his son Jamal is 16 now".

"And how is Jamal's crazy mother?"

"Still crazy, but she relinquished custody so Jamal, lives with Kevin and Tasha".

"Mikki, please if you can get them over there have Tasha and Kevin over for brunch as well, it would be nice to see most of my friends while we are in town".

"Will do. I will even call Zavier, Dez and Leslie and Tim and ask them to come over." "I'll make the arrangements so we can get some spades going and the grill on the deck while you guys are here".

"That would be great for all of us to get together; we haven't done it in so long".

"I'll let you go, but I will definitely call you later in the week". Mikki hung up the phone and made her way through the family room to go upstairs to the master suite so that she could go and take a nap. As soon as she got to the top of the steps, the phone rang.

"Hello, oh, hi you doing Mikki, is my son around?"

"No, he's not here right now. Oh, could you please ask him to call me when he gets in?"

"Sure no problem". After hanging up with her mother in law, Mikki stretched out across her bed and reminisced about her wedding day to James and how it was almost ruined.

Mikki smiled as the photographer took pictures of her mother sliding on her garter. After putting on her garter, her mother helped her with her veil and they walked down the stairs where her bridesmaids, her brothers and her father waited for her. This was the day that Mikki had always dreamed of, and she was sure that James was her prince charming.

Mikki had a relatively big wedding party; Michele was her maid of honor, Gina was her matron of honor (due to her and Mike's quickie shotgun wedding 2 years ago), her sisters, Jamie, Monica and Leslie were her bridesmaids, MJ and her nephew Brandon were the ring bearers, and Kayla and her two nieces Bianca and Brittany were the flower girls. When Mikki finally got to the bottom of the stairs, she saw the tears in the eyes of her sisters and her sister friends.

"Look ladies, you cannot cry right now, if I see you cry then, I will cry and mess up my makeup before I see James".

Her sister Jamie walked over to her and dabbed Mikki's eyes for her. "You look so beautiful big sis, I am so happy for you!"

"Well, let's get going guys I know that we only have to go around the corner to the church but, I want to at least start on time".

They all headed out of the house where the bridesmaids , the ring bearers and the flower girls got into one limo, Mikki's parents got into the Rolls Royce along with Mikki and the wedding coordinator, Mikki's brothers, Gina and Michele got into the other Limo. When they got to the church, Mikki's parents got out of the car and let Mikki stay outside until they were ready for her. Mikki took a deep breath; everything will go off without a hitch. Mikki caught a glimpse of James' half sister Janice and her mother Joyce rush up the steps of the church with Janice's husband Mark. She then saw Zavier's car pull up and out jumped James' mother and his sister Regina and Regina's best friend and sidekick Melissa get out. Because the Rolls Royce that Mikki was sitting in windows were tinted, they could not see her sitting in the back.

"Come on Miss Gina, the wedding is about to start, and I have to get inside so that I can escort Mikki's sister down the aisle".

" Well, Zavier, thank you for picking us up and bringing us here, but I just can't understand why no one made arrangements for us to have a limo to get to the wedding".

"Miss Gina, please you have to get inside to walk down the aisle with Jackson because you are parents of the groom". "Please don't let James down this is his special day".

" I'm coming Zavier, Rita you make sure that you and Melissa get in here and sit down, I know that James' godmother is here and she can make sure that you guys get to the reception".

"We will just give us a minute!"

Mikki just shook her head, *please lord, please do not let anyone ruin my day.* Just then, Mikki heard *Overjoyed,* by Stevie Wonder playing and new that the James' parents were being seated. Mikki breathed a sigh of relief. She then heard Ribbon in the sky and new that her mother and grandmother was being escorted down the aisle by her brothers.

Just then Margaret the wedding coordinator opened the car door and told Mikki that is was time to come into the church. She stepped out the car and looked around to see if anyone was going to see her before she made her grand entrance in the church. She walked up the steps as Margaret held up the back of her dress. The usher opened the outside door and she saw her father standing there smiling. He walked over to her and grabbed her arms. She could hear the Wedding Song by Kenny G playing and she knew that the rest of the bridal party was walking in. She caught a glimpse of her brothers pulling the runner down the aisle and at the same time saying the bride is coming, the bride is coming.

She smiled, her dad put the veil over her face and they both turned to begin proceeding down the aisle. The usher opened the door and *"We Must be in Love"* by Pure Soul began playing. Mikki smiled at the first people she saw who occupied the back rows in the church. The photographer told her to wait one second as he took a picture of her and her dad in the door way. She continued the walk and could see that James had a big smile on his face as he waited for her with the pastor at the altar. Mikki thought to herself, my dream wedding and she knew that everything was right.

Her bridesmaids were dressed in cream taffeta wrap dresses that were accentuated with cranberry and cream bows at the waist, that because they were iridescent, when different colored lights hit the gowns they picked up the color from the lights. Her maid and matron of honor both wore cranberry sleeveless wrap dresses that were also iridescent and accentuated with cream bows at the waist. The flower girls all wore, cream dresses that had iridescent cranberry sashes and cranberry ribbons in there Shirley temple curled pig tails.

All of the bridesmaids carried bouquets of star gazer lilies and all of the groomsmen had the same type of flowers pinned to their lapels. Mikki's grandmother was given 4 white roses, Mikki's mother was carrying star gazer lilies and James' mother was given a small bouquet of white lilies. Mikki's bouquet was the ultimate of all. She had a bouquet of white calla lilies that had a few of the star gazer lilies to maintain her theme of cranberry, crème and white.

When she got to the altar, Mikki smiled at James and lipped I love you. He smiled and their ceremony began. The wedding went on without a hitch, they had a dance tribute while the soloist sang, the Lord's prayer and Send a Revival. They said there I Do's and nobody stood up to say why they should not be married and they were pronounced, Mr. and Mrs. James Stevens. Mikki was ecstatic, she had married her dream man, she had a good wedding day and it was now time to go and party!

The wedding party was led out of the sanctuary by the tribute dancers and into the foyer to set up the receiving line. Mikki saw her mother go over and talk to Jackson and Regina to let them know that they would stand in the receiving line as well. When they got in to their places in the receiving line, Mikki put a smile on her face and gently squeezed James's hand, she was so happy and he looked over and smiled at her.

The first people to come through the receiving line were Joyce, James' stepmother. She whispered hello to James and gave him a kiss on the cheek and she stood in front of Mikki and just took in the whole picture. "Mikki you look so beautiful she said. I am so glad to welcome you into the family and now Janice has that sister close to her age like she always wanted".

"Thank you Joyce".

They preceded on and said hello to all of the family and friends that came to celebrate their special day. Once, they were finished with the receiving line, Margaret their coordinator designated who would drive in what cars as they drove to the Art Museum to take pictures. They had exactly 2 hours before their reception started at the Wyndham Franklin Plaza at 17th and race streets in Philadelphia. That would give them just enough time to go to their bridal suite and for Mikki to change her dress into the sleeker dress that she purchased for the reception.

Mikki drove in the Rolls Royce with James and the children. The groomsmen, Mikki's brothers, and her parents drove in one limo and the bridesmaids and James' mother Regina and his father Jackson were to ride in another. Before Regina could actually get in the car, she got into an argument with Rita because Rita thought that she was going to ride in the limo with her mother.

James sighed, "I knew that something like this was going to happen!"

"Rita, go and get in the car with Darlene and Spencer, they will take you to the reception and Zavier will give you a ride home".

"Mom, you said that I would be able to ride in the limo with you!"

James walked over to where Rita was and grabbed her by the arm. "Rita, go get in the car with Darlene and Spencer, you cannot ride in the limo". "You are a grown woman, act like it!" Rita sulked and snatched her arm out of James' grasp. She rolled her eyes and walked over to get in the car.

Mikki then realized that she was holding her breath and breathed a sigh of relief and they were off to take pictures at the Art Museum. Once at the art museum they took pictures in the gazebo overlooking the water and headed to the hotel.

Once in the bridal suite, she asked Margaret to assist the bridal party with drinks and such so she could change her clothes. She and James went to the adjoining suite so that they could change their clothes for the reception.

"James, I am so happy".

"I know you are sweetie. You look so beautiful in that dress, your cleavage is off the hook!"

"James you pervert! Why do I have to be a pervert? I am just looking at my wife and I definitely cannot wait to get to know you on our honeymoon if you know what I mean?"

"Well, James for right now, let's just enjoy our reception and you'll have to wait to see what I have in store for you for the honeymoon!"

James smiled and went to the closet to pull out the cream linen pants and matching shirt that he planned on wearing to the reception.

He helped Mikki unzip her dress and kissed her on her neck. She held up the front of her dress and walked over to where she had laid out her linen strapless dress for the reception. James watched her lower her dress and smiled seductively at her sexy undergarments. He walked over and grabbed her dress and laid it across the chaise lounge so that she could put on her other dress. After they both were changed they went back in the suite where everyone was waiting, it was time for them to go up to the Horizon ballroom to party the night away.

When they got to the ballroom, they waited outside so that the wedding party could be introduced. After introductions of the rest of the bridal party, the doors opened and Mikki saw Rita running towards her with a glass of juice that she splashed in her face.

Mikki screamed, "What is wrong with you Rita, why would you do something like that?"

"Because, I don't like you bitch! I am so tired of you acting like you are better than me". James grabbed Rita's arm, "What is on your mind? Why would you do something like try and ruin my wedding day?"

Just then Margaret the wedding coordinator and Mikki's cousin Taylor came running over with towels to help Mikki wipe her face. Mikki tried to laugh off the situation but inside she really wanted to cry.

"I guess she wanted to welcome me to the family?"

Mikki's parents came over and stood with Mikki while James argued with Rita and his mother at the other end of the hallway. Mikki tried to decipher what was being said but couldn't. After about 5 minutes, James came back down the hall and told Margaret to introduce them and hugged Mikki and told her everything was going to be alright. But Mikki had a feeling it was never going to be alright.

After partying until about midnight with their guests, James and Mikki retired to their suite. They were both glad that their flight to Aruba would not be until Monday morning, so they could rest at the hotel all day Sunday and bask in being husband and wife.

"Mikki, I am glad that you booked our honeymoon from Monday to Monday, it will give us time to relax and not have to rush to get to the airport tomorrow morning or have to get up early".

"Yeah, I'm glad too".

James put his arm around her and kissed her on neck. "Baby, I just want to give you the world. You are so special to me. I'm sorry for my stupid sister; she's just a stupid kid who refuses to grow up".

"Mikki put her hands to his lips, look James, don't make excuses for your sister, I don't want to talk about it, and we are going to enjoy our honeymoon starting now".

She pulled him into the bedroom to show that while they were enjoying their reception, she had planned something special for him. On the table, there was a bottle of Moet and two glasses and on the bed were rose petals, she had laid on the bed cranberry silk boxers for him and a matching cranberry silk night gown and robe for her.

"I am going to change, Mr. Stevens, and I will see you when I come back!"

James smiled and began changing in to his boxers while she went into the bathroom to change. When Mikki came out of the bathroom, he smiled at her. She walked over to the table and poured two glasses of Moet and brought them over to where James stood.

"To us, Mr. Stevens. James removed the glass from her hand and pulled her close to him. He gently kissed her on the lips and then made his way down her neck. He took off her robe and let it fall to the floor and laid her on the bed. He then kissed her while caressing her neck. He then caressed her nipple and took the right one into his mouth. He then reached down and lifted up her gown and raised it above her head to see that she was wearing a matching cranberry thong. He then continued to caress her right nipple as he continued his escapade of kissing every part of her body. He lingered for a while just above her hip and then began kissing her thighs. He removed her thong and turned her over and kissed her back, while Mikki arched and let out a low moan.

James turned her back over and slowly kissed the nape of her neck, shoulders in between her breasts and her belly button with all intentions of savoring every last drop.

He then reached between her legs and could feel the swell of emotion and anticipation that she had for him. He blew softly across her woman hood and playfully licked her with his tongue. He then grabbed her by the hips and continued to work his magic until shudders of orgasmic pleasure waved throughout her whole body. He pulled her to him and they made love for hours.

The next morning, the two of them ordered room service and just lay around for most of the day. They read the Sunday paper and watched television and just stayed huddled in bed. Around 2pm, they received a call from Mikki's parents to see how they were doing and to let them know to expect a gift basket to be delivered later. They decided to have dinner at the hotel's restaurant but they also decided that they would call Gina, Mike, Zavier, Janice, Chris and Michele to join them.

After having a nice dinner with their friends, they retired to their room, where Mikki noticed that they had messages waiting.

"James could you please check the messages? I want to jump in the shower before we go to bed and make sure that we are all packed for tomorrow".

"Sure honey, I will check the messages, they are probably from Michele to let us know that they were downstairs waiting for us earlier". Mikki grabbed the clothes out of the bathroom and returned to watch frustration arise on James' face.

"What's wrong honey? It's my mom, she said that this morning, Rita left the house this morning and left Diamond and Sierra with Jordan and little Russell. Russell is out looking for her now, but my mother is extremely upset because this has happened before".

Mikki went over to James and hugged him. "I'm sorry that this happened James, do you want me to call Chris and have him come back and get you so that you can go out and look for her?"

" I was just about to do that, are you going to be okay, Mik?"

"Yes, I know this is your family and our flight is for 10am tomorrow morning which means that we have to be at the airport by 8 am. If anyone can find your sister, it is definitely you".

James picked up the phone and called his brother Chris who said that he would be there to pick him up in about 20 minutes. He changed out of his slacks that he wore to dinner and put on a pair of jeans and a t-shirt and headed towards the door with Mikki right behind him.

"Mikki, I thought you were going to stay here? No, I am going with you to help you find your sister and get her back home".

They both took the stairs and walked out of the 17th street entrance to wait for Chris to pull up. Once in the car, they drove south on 17th street until they got to Washington avenue and made a left onto Washington Avenue. They followed Washington Avenue until they got to 13th street and made another left. Once they made the left they followed 13th street until they got to Catherine Street where they saw a group of people standing outside of a round building. There was a flurry of activity going on. Guys were playing dice, some were just standing around drinking 40's, you had crowds of people of all ages just hanging out and going in and out of this building. Chris pulled over the car and parked near the corner. James and Mikki got out of the car and walked in the direction of the building.

James said to Chris, "there she is!" Chris yelled, "Yo Rita, get over here!"

Rita turned around and frowned.

"Get over here now!"

Rita walked over to where Chris, James and Mikki stood.

"What is on your mind? Why would you leave your children at home and just decide to not come home at all? Rita, you are 20 years old you have two daughters at home that need you as a role model and you're down here chasing after your baby daddy! Answer me!"

"James, leave me alone, I was not down here chasing after Sean. I came down here to hang out and just chill".

Chris looked at her and frowned. "Girl don't you know that your chillin' days are over? You being able to hang out with your friends all day is not what you are supposed to be doing. You need to be responsible for your girls, Rita".

Mikki shook her head in agreement with Chris and James.

Rita turned to her, "What do you have to say about this Miss Bourgeois goody two shoes? "What you decided to come for the ride, so that you could look down your nose even further? What so you can run back to your little friends that were in your wedding and tell them how ghetto, James' sister is?"

"Rita, I don't talk about you that often, because family business is not something that I tend to spread around to my friends".

"Family, we're not family, you just married my brother and I really cannot stand you that much, like I told you yesterday, Bitch!"

"Rita, you apologize to Mikki right now, I will not sit here and let you disrespect her like that".

Mikki turned around and went back to the car before Rita could even garner an apology. James grabbed Rita by the arm and took her back to the car and made her sit in the back seat with him. They safely delivered her to his mom's house where when they pulled up, Russell was sitting outside on the steps smoking a cigarette. Rita got out of the car and walked past her father and into the house.

"Russell, why aren't you out looking for Rita? I was, but when your mother told me that she called you, I just decided that I would chill out".

"Chill out? You're her father, why would you stop looking for her? I stopped because, I knew that the almighty, James would come to everyone's rescue and he would bring Rita home".

James was furious and Chris knew it, he grabbed his arm. "Come on bro, let's just get you back to the hotel so that you can rest and go on your honeymoon".

James shook his head and walked away from his mother's house and got back in the car so that he could resume enjoying be a newlywed.

James

James opened the garage and smiled. He had tired out Steven and Scott by taking them to Rainbow playground and playing whatever they wanted to play. When he told them that they had to leave, they were disappointed but they also knew that dinner was going to be served soon. He parked his truck and helped the boys climb out. When they walked into the kitchen, they saw Mikki placing everything on the table so that they could sit down for dinner. Skylar, Shannon and Jason were sitting on the floor in the family room watching the Proud Family.

"Okay, guys, wash your hands, so that we can sit down to dinner". They all ran into the powder room and washed their hands. "No shoving guys, James added".

"Honey everything smells good and I'm starving".

"Well, go and wash your hands Mr. Stevens so that we can sit down together as a family".

After dinner, Mikki went into her office and packed her briefcase with things she needed to take to work. She then went into the kitchen to load the dishwasher and wipe off the counters, while James made sure that all of the kids had taken their showers and get into their pajamas. The kids tried to protest, but they all knew that 8 o'clock was there bedtime. After an hour of watching television downstairs, James grabbed two wine glasses out of the cabinet and grabbed a bottle of Mikki's favorite merlot out of the wine cabinet and sat it in the wine cooler on a tray and went upstairs in their master suite. He knew what he had in mind, he was going to seduce and thank his wife for allowing them to become a family again. When he opened the door to the master suite, Mikki was just coming out of the shower and was wrapped in her bathrobe.

"So what do you have on your mind, Mr. Stevens?"

"You, you and thanking you".

Mikki smiled, she would never tell him, but she definitely had make up sex on her mind as well.

James took the tray with the wine and placed it on the table in their sitting room. Mikki walked to her walk in closet and pulled out her cranberry night gown and matching thong. She slipped them on and saw that James had put on his cranberry sleep pants and was sitting at their café table with the wine already poured. Mikki sat down across from him and picked up her glass.

"To us, and maintaining a loving and solid marriage from now on".

"No, to you for being honest with me and making me see the light as far as what should be first in my life, and that's you and the kids". He stood up and placed his glass on the table between them.

He then walked over to the CD player that was in their entertainment armoire and put on *This Time I'll be Sweeter* by Angela Bofill and pulled Mikki into an embrace and began to slow dance with her. He then ran his fingers thru her hair and kissed her on the neck. She then began caressing his strong arms and back and they continued to sway. He then picked her up and walked over to their king size bed and laid her on her back. He then sat next to her and lowered her night gown so that he could look at her breasts. He began to squeeze both of her nipples and reached down and kissed each one. He ran his tongue across her collarbone and down the valley between her breasts. He gently removed her nightgown and the matching thong.

He looked her lovingly in the eyes and whispered, I love you in ear. He kissed her elbows, her side and slid down to the valley of her woman hood and breathed slow deep breaths. He massaged her thighs to prepare her for the sensual strokes that he was going to use to devour every inch of her. He took his left hand and stroked her feminity with precise motions.

Mikki let out a sigh as he began to stroke her with his tongue. With every stroke he milked her faster and faster until he heard her moan his name. He straddled her and began to tease her by putting his manhood in the swell of her and taking it out. Mikki bucked against him every time until she could not stand the tease anymore. Mikki grabbed his hip and guided him to the most erotic pleasure he ever had. She moved her hips to his rhythm and wrapped her legs around him to balance her. He placed his hands behind her and lifted her slightly off the bed until they both climaxed together. He laid her gently on the bed and brushed her hair out of her face and kissed her on the cheek.

"I love you James, and I always will", Mikki said.

"I love you too, Mrs. Stevens and I want you to know that you mean everything to me and I could not face losing you again". He then grabbed her and they both went to get in the shower before returning to bed again.

Mikki

Mikki walked into her office the next morning, with a big smile on her face. She remembered last night events with her husband and was glad that for now they were getting along and the demon had not reared its ugly head yet. She knew that any day now, something would come up and it would be a test to see how James would handle it. She looked down at her desk to look at her schedule and added the entry to make sure that she called her lawyer to give her the updates on what was happening with her and James. Just then her phone rang and because her secretary was not due until 9, she had to answer it.

"Hello, Mikki Stevens".

"Hello, Mikki, this is your mother, calling to see how you and the grand babies are doing?"

"Hi Mom, we are all fine, but I since we haven't talked in the last two weeks, I have to let you know that James is back home".

" Well, isn't that interesting, I knew that you had taken the kids on a special weekend trip and you have the New Jersey museum trip coming up soon, but I did not know that you were back to living in the same house. That's good Mik. I'm glad that you stopped blaming all of your problems on your mother in law".

"Now, Mom, you know that was not what I was doing. I just did not want to play second fiddle to her and the problems going on at her house". "Dad never put you second to anyone, not even us".

"Well sweetie, you cannot compare, your relationship with James to me and your father's – that's two different time periods and two different age groups".

"Oh, mom you know what I mean and I know you did not call to give me a big dissertation on my marriage".

"No Mik, you are right, I called to let you know that Sandra wanted me to call you and ask if you would be in your brother's wedding as a bridesmaid".

"Oh, so when were they going to tell me that they had decided on a date? I knew that they were engaged, but Sandra told me she would let me know because they planned on having a long engagement".

" Well, they can't have a long engagement now, we just found out that Sandra is expecting and is due in approximately 7 months, so Joey wants to get married before the baby is born".

"Well, I will call her later and give my congratulations and I will definitely be a bridesmaid".

"Joey asked Mark to be his best man and Sandra is not planning on wearing white". "She said that she did not plan on wearing white at all". "Her favorite color is blue, so she wanted to wear a light pastel blue dress anyway".

"Well, mom, I have to go but I will definitely call Sandra tonight to see if she needs any help from me". "Kiss Dad for me and I will give you a call a little later".

Mikki hung up the phone and pull papers out of her brief case to review the information for the family meeting that she had coming up this morning. She had completed a new intake for a child to come to her school and she had to review the Individual Education Plan so that she understood what services this new child would need if the family decided that the child would attend her school and if they could meet the needs of the child at their site.

Just then a delivery person rang the door bell. She could see that he was carrying an edible fruit basket where the fruit was arranged like flowers. She smiled, I guess Pam, got another delivery from the smooth talking guy she's dating. She opened the door and signed for the package and placed it on the secretary's desk and returned to her office to finish preparing for her upcoming meeting.

When Pam came in at 9 o'clock, she said good morning and put coffee on because she knew that the therapist would ask for her special brew during this meeting. Pam also brought in pastries from Romano's bakery near her home in Overbrook. Pam noticed the fruit basket on her desk and read the card. After reading the card, she picked up the fruit basket and knocked on Mikki's office door.

"Come in!"

"Mik, you left these on my desk, but these are not for me, there for you".

"Me?" " You must be kidding Pam". "Who would send me a fruit basket?" " Definitely, not James, he is not the flower type, he's too macho for that, he is more the type to say, I paid the mortgage, I did something special for you".

"Pam laughed, sorry boss lady but these are for you".

Mikki took the fruit basket to her desk and smiled. She picked up her phone and dialed James' cell phone because she knew that he was on his way to work after dropping off the twins and Jason at Kindercare.

"Hello, James Stevens speaking".

"Hi babe, it's Mikki, I was just calling to say thank you for the fruit basket. I really love it".

"I'm glad babe, I just left the kids and I plan on heading to Philly to take my mother to her doctor's appointment and they try to catch up with one of the technicians at the Pitney Bowes site to help him with a problem that he is having there".

"Oh, Mikki sighed". She thought to herself, *here we go again, running errands for momma.* His mother could have easily just taken the bus to her doctor's appointment, but she would not dare say anything to him. James must have recognized the reservation in Mikki's voice so he told her that he had already told his mother that he would take her and he would make sure that he was home before dinner.

"I love you Mikki, I would not let anything come between us, we need to work on us, and I know that now".

"I love you too, babe. I have to go because I have a meeting soon and I still need to review my paperwork so that I am prepared".

"Okay, babe, I will talk to you soon". Mikki hung up the phone, but could not help but wonder how much more his mother was going to do that day.

The rest of Mikki's day went relatively smoothly, the children in the early intervention program went on a trip to Linvilla Orchard and the older children in the support program were having an assembly. Mikki decided to leave work early and go home to see James before they had to pick up the children from Kindercare at 5:30. She looked at her watch and knew that James would already be at home probably in their basement working out. He made a habit of trying to work out at least 3 times a week and the home gym in their basement made that possible.

When she got home and opened the garage door on her side, she saw that James car was there as she expected. She parked her car and grabbed her briefcase and entered the house through the mud room. When she entered the house she heard laughter and voices coming from the basement.

"James, is that you?" She opened the basement door and to her surprise, she saw her two brothers in laws, Jordan and Russell.

"Oh hi guys, is James downstairs?"

"Yes he's right here".

Mikki walked down the steps and saw that not only were her brother in laws there, so were her mother in law Regina, her sister in law Rita and Rita's two little girls.

"Hello everyone", Mikki said coolly. James' nieces said hello, but Rita and Regina said nothing. James came over to Mikki and kissed her on the cheek then looked from his mother and his sister to see why they had not spoken to Mikki.

Mikki then decided that she would not make a scene but she would go upstairs and change her clothes so that she could go and pick the kids up. James followed her upstairs in order to talk to her for a minute.

"Mikki, I know you were not expecting them to be here but, after I took my mom to her doctor's appointment, Rita asked if I could take her to Aston to look at an apartment on Pennel road". "She seems to be trying to do something with herself and stop free loading off my mother and Russell. My mother gave her the down payment which was about $1500 and is planning on buying her some furniture and she has a job at the Dollar store across the street from her apartment we just came from there and everything is set".

"Well, I am happy for all of them James, but I think it is quite rude for your mother and your sister not to speak and you did not say anything to either one of them. They are in my home and they can at least show me respect".

"I know babe, please don't make a scene".

"That's all you're worried about James? I think it would be more important for you to take a stand for me where they both are concerned. That's okay, I'm a big girl, and I can take it". "Although you took those vows to love honor and respect me, you don't want to hurt your mom's feelings".

"But Mikki"

"James it is okay, I see you haven't learned anything from us being separated". "I am your wife and whatever your mother and sister do to me, you should take it as they are doing it to you – but you have let them walk over and take advantage of you for so many years that you think it's the norm".

"Mikki!"

"Leave me alone James, go back to entertaining your family, I will go about doing what I need to do for mine!"

James returned to his family in the basement and decided that it was time to take them home. He would have a talk with Mikki later.

James

The drive to take his mother and the rest of his family back home gave him a headache. All his mother could do was complain about how rude Mikki was and how she came in prancing through the house like she was a queen. Rita added fuel to her mother's fire by stating that she never liked Mikki because she thought she was better than them. Jordan and Russell just sat in the back of James's SUV and did not say a word. After he dropped them off, James decided that he had time to stop by and see his in-laws and maybe talk to his father in law to see if he could make sense of all of this. When he pulled up to the house he saw that his brother in law Mark and his current girlfriend Jasmine were going in the house. He parked his car and used his key to unlock the screen door and went in. When he went in he saw that Mikki's brother in law Tim was there with their youngest boy Trevor.

"Hey everybody, wassup?" " Man, Tim Trevor is getting bigger and bigger every day". "How are those little women doing?"

"Well, Tanya is playing basketball, Tamara is playing volleyball, and Tia is dancing, playing softball, basketball and volleyball- so you know Leslie and I have our hands full".

"Well, I know that you guys have your hands full with 3 soon to be teenagers!" "Well kiss the T sisters and Leslie for me. Is dad around?"

"Yes he is tinkering with the grill in the back, and I think Mark smelled food so that's why he and Jasmine are here".

James laughed. He made his way to the back yard and saw that his mother in law was sitting in the back yard as well talking to her sister who happened to be in town for the week. "Hello ladies", James said as he stepped out of the screen door and onto the deck. "Dad, can I talk to you for a minute?"

His father in law did not look his age, or look like he was ready to retire from the School District. At 60, and no visible signs of grey head, Mikki's father could pass for at least 40. He was as tall as James, with a slightly dark mahogany complexion and dark brown eyes that would move you to tell the truth. Due to his years as a star athlete and a middle school principal he had kept relatively in shape to chase some of the delinquents at his school.

"Sure, ladies would you excuse me please?" "Mom, I have started the grill so if you want to put the lamb on first you can and I will check it when I finish talking with my son".

They both went back into the house and made their way to his make shift den which was situated between the dining room and the living room and shut the sliding doors.

"So take a seat son what's on your mind?"

"Well, dad, you know that Mikki and I separated and I am now back at home but I don't feel that we have moved passed the breaking point". "I've hurt Mikki by not making a decision when she gave me the ultimatum, and she only let me come back home because, she knew that the kids really missed me". "I don't want to mess this up; I want for her to believe that I respect her and wouldn't put anything before her".

"Well, son, I have to tell you that you know how stubborn, my daughter can be, she gets it from both her mother and me and she has a lot a pride". "The one thing that I do know is that she loves you with all of her heart". "If you don't understand why she is so upset with you, then I think that maybe you need to go to counseling". "Specifically I would not go to counseling at the church but maybe some type of mediation where the person is objective and can give you more insight on what Mikki is feeling".

"But, dad, you know that I am a very private person, I cannot see going to a shrink and have them tell me that I am a bad husband and that Mikki is right".

"That's not what I said son, I am saying mediation, someone who is objective who can make you listen and understand Mikki's thought process and why she has gotten to this point". "I think at the University of Penn they have a counseling center, so maybe you should look that up and see what you and Mikki could possibly arrange".

"Thanks Dad, I will think about it. I can't stay that long, I have to be home for dinner in about ½ an hour and I don't want to be penalized for that". James got up and shook his father in laws hand and headed out the door. On his way out he said goodnight to his mother in law and her sister, Mark, Tim, Trevor and Jasmine. In the car on the way home, he thought a lot about what his father in law had to say and made up his mind that he had to at least give this counseling thing a chance.

Mikki grabbed her briefcase and was readying herself to leave work. This weekend she had made plans with James and some of her friends to go skiing at Jack Frost and they had rented a cabin instead of staying at the lodge. She looked at her watch and saw that she had enough time before she was to meet James at his apartment to go and get a manicure and a pedicure. Her and James had been hot and heavy for approximately 4 months now. She did not think that it was serious just yet, but she did like him and they spent a lot of time together. She went out to her car and placed her briefcase in the trunk and she headed for the nearest salon so that she could get her manicure and pedicure done.

After getting her nails done she headed to her apartment so that she could pack her stuff for their weekend ski trip. Mikki opened her apartment door, pick up the mail off the floor and dropped it on her kitchen table and headed to the answering machine to listen to her messages.

"Beep- Hey girl, it's Gina, Mike and I will stop by your house to pick you up so be ready. Zavier and his girlfriend Sasha will meet us at the cabin because he is driving down from New York and Michele will be bringing Anthony. Well kisses honey and we will see you around 6".

"Beep- Hey babe, its James and I just wanted to call and let you know that I'm thankful that you planned this weekend for us to celebrate my birthday and to hang out with our friends. I love you and I will see you soon.

Mikki thought to herself that James was so sweet. She grabbed her ski pants out of the closet and grabbed her weekender bag and made sure that she had everything ready for this weekend. About an hour later, she heard her bell and knew that it had to be Gina and Mike picking her up. She opened the door and gave Mike and Gina both a hug.

"Hey girl, are you ready to go?"

" Yes, please tell me that you are not taking as much time as, this lady over here and please say that you do not have as much luggage!"

"Mike, are you over reacting again?" You and Gina have been a couple for how long, and you haven't gotten the gist of her designer labels and shoes to match?"

"Look, I don't have a problem with my woman looking good, but it's my back that is catching the brunt of it!"

The three of them laughed. Mikki turned on her answering machine and grabbed her keys off the coffee table and grabbed her bag. I'm ready to go. They all headed out of her apartment and headed to Mike's Ford Explorer. Once in the car they headed from Mikki's apartment into the city and they were all relieved that traffic was not that bad on the way. They pulled up at James apartment in less the 15 minutes flat. They parked up the street from James' apartment building and headed toward his door.

James must have seen them from his front window because when they reached the door, they were all buzzed in. James met them at the top of the steps holding his cordless phone to his ear.

"Yo, James wassup man? Are you ready to go?"

James shook his head but continued to listen to whomever he was talking to. They followed him into his apartment and the girls sat on his futon which was supposed to be his couch and Mike went straight to the refrigerator in his small kitchen. After a few more minutes of his one sided conversation, James hung up the phone and let out a sigh.

Gina looked up and asked," What's wrong James?"

Mikki and Mike looked at James to see what his response was going to be, he had a tired look on his face but deep in his eyes you saw anger and increasing frustration.

James let a deep sigh, "Well folks, that was my mother, she is upset that I will not be able to pick her up from work tonite because we are going skiing, I was just basically listening to her rant and rave about me shirking my family duties to her. She is also upset that I did not talk to my sister Rita about her flunking grades. Rita just had Diamond, her little girl 5 weeks ago, and they just got her grades from the school for pregnant teenagers and they are not great at all. I told her that I would talk to Rita, but my new responsibilities at my job since my supervisor left have left me tired when I get home from work, not to mention that I am constantly called upon to take them shopping at a moments notice".

Gina walked over to James and gave him a hug and said, that she hoped that things would turn around for him soon. Mike just shook his head and said nothing.

Mikki frowned but chose her words carefully before saying anything to James about the situation. "James, I know that it is important for you to be there for your family but you are your mother's child and some things need to be handled by her and your step dad Russell".

"I know Mikki, but since I am the oldest son and she and Russell did not get married until Jordan was born and I was 16 I had to be the man of the house, I made sure the kids were fed when they came home for school, I did the food shopping, I was the disciplinarian because for a long time my mother worked different shifts at the hospital. I know that I have left home, but I still feel responsible to do my part".

"Man, I know that you feel that you have to do your part, but don't you think Russell should be taking on those responsibilities? Mike said.

"In a way, I do believe that, but he has not stepped up to the plate like he should and that leaves my mom scrambling to get things done, especially now because Rita has Diamond and that is another mouth to feed".

"Well, what exactly did she say to you?"

"She has to work 11pm to 7 am tonite and then double back at 3pm tomorrow afternoon so that she can have Monday off, to take Diamond to a doctor's appointment. I told her that I asked my father to pick her up tonight and when I spoke with my dad, he said that he would take her and pick her up on both days. She was upset about having to be around my father because of all the animosity that they have for one another".

"I would think that she would be grateful that you went to those lengths to make other arrangements for her, but I see that is not good enough", Gina said.

"It is giving me a headache to think that she would depend on you to make arrangements for her, she's a grown woman", Mike said.

"Well, now that we had this discussion, can we head out so that we can hit the slopes, bright and early", Mikki said. Her head was spinning and she did not want to have to deal with this on their weekend. And to top it all off, she had a surprise waiting for James at the cabin they had rented for the weekend for his birthday.

Mikki grabbed his arm, "come on James, it's your 25th birthday this weekend, let's just go and have fun". James smiled at Mikki and went and into his bedroom and grabbed his duffle bag off of the bed and turned off the lights.

"Yeah, let's go have some fun!"

It took them 2 hours to get to the cabin in the Poconos, when they pulled up they did not see Zavier or Michele's car but Mike had gotten his key for the cabin and let them in. Mike ran back to the car and told James to go in and that he would handle getting the rest of the bags out of his truck.

When James walked into the cabin, the lights unexpectedly came on and a whole group of people yelled surprise! James clutched his chest to imitate that he was going to have a heart attack but then he looked around and saw all of his friends and was extremely excited.

Mikki, Mike and Gina walked in and screamed gotcha! James was extremely happy, no one had ever gone the lengths that Mikki did to plan this surprise for him. He started to greet people and was glad to see that his sister Janice was there with her husband Derek, Mikki's sister Leslie and her husband Tim, his brother Chris and his wife Charmaine, some of his fraternity brothers and their significant others, some of his cousins and uncles as well.

James walked over to Mikki and grabbed her and kissed her on the cheek, "Thanks babe, I really appreciate this, this is going to be something, I never forget". "How did you pull this off?"

"Well, I had called Janice to see if she wanted to go skiing with us for this weekend and when I called, Charmaine was there visiting so we hatched the plan". "Chris found this group of cabins that all had at least 3 bedrooms in each and got a deal on them so, Janice booked all of them on her credit card and we went from there". "Mike, called most of your frat brothers, I knew that Zavier and Michele would love to go and then I just got other phone numbers out of your phone book and started calling people". "For the people that I thought, I wouldn't feel comfortable calling, I asked Janice to call and it was a done deal".

"You are really popular, young man", Gina said when she walked over and handed Mike a beer.

The night went on without a hitch, Zavier and Michele's friend Anthony had started up the grill and Chris and Mike brought out trays of hor d'oeurves. The night went on for hours and the best thing about the party was that everyone had their own cabin to retire to.

The next morning everyone in their party was up early and ready to hit the slopes. There was a caravan of cars leaving their cabins and headed to the lodge. Once there, they all got skis and headed to the slopes. James made sure that he stayed close to Mikki because she was till an amateur when it came to skiing. They all skied for 4 hours and they all decided that they would go to eat at one of the fast food restaurants and after they ate, the ladies would hook up for a shopping trip at the out let mall and the guys would go bowling.

Once they got to the mall Janice pulled Mikki to the side to have a brief conversation with her.

"So, Janice, what's on your mind?"

"Mikki, I just wanted to thank you for being so thoughtful about my brother's birthday".

"Well, Janice, I believe that he would have done it for me, so why not do it for him?" "I really care about James, and rest assured we are taking it very slowly and I for sure don't jump into things too quickly".

"That's not what I wanted to talk you about at all". "Mikki, I know that you have a special place in my brother's heart and we have become good friends since the two of you started dating and friend to friend, I just want to tell you to watch out for his mother and sister". "I know that they are a pair of leeches and no mother and sister should be as dependent on him like they are".

"My mother has seen it and always told James to watch out for it because she loves him like he was her own". "I want you to be careful, with your heart and be careful of Regina and Rita".

Mikki frowned, "Janice I will heed your advice but you know that, one of the qualities that attracted me to your brother was the way he made sure that his mother and her family was taken care of".

"Yes, I know Janice answered, but, Regina is married and her husband should be taking on those duties". "When Derek and I went to counseling before we got married, our pastor told us that when we get married, we become one and that no one should come between the family that you make". "You and James are not married, but Regina is and all of the things that she asks James to do is what Russell should be doing". "My mother always worried that as a teenager, James took on to much responsibility". "Regina placed that responsibility with him". "In a way that is why I think that Russell always makes snide remarks to James".

"I read this article in a magazine not too long ago, about Black women who raise their sons to be the man that they want them to be, but they tend to cause trouble for their sons when they begin to date". "The article said that a study used 100 single mothers whose oldest children were sons and took a look at how they raised them and what responsibility these young men were given. 75 percent of these women said in their interviews that when their sons got older, that they tried to sabotage relationships by demanding a lot of time from their sons, or telling their sons that the women that they were dating were not good enough for them to keep them from getting married". "60 percent of the mothers studied were happy that if their sons did get married that the marriages did not last and at least they had grandchildren out of the relationships".

Mikki looked at Janice with awe but did not quickly respond.

"All I am saying is that, I have seen my brother date some nice girls who headed for the door because of his mother and sister and I hope that you are not one of them".

"Janice, that has yet to be seen, I'm strong but I really don't believe that his mother would really try and sabotage our relationship or James would let her for that matter".

"Well, you've been warned. Now let's get over to Nine West and see what they have on sale!" They both laughed and headed towards the store.

James laughed at Zavier when his missed his shot while they were playing pool.

"Man, you have really lost your touch man". "And I see old smooth talker James really put his mack down if Mikki is making arrangements and throwing weekend birthday parties".

"Look man, Mikki and I are taking things slowly, she is my main girl but it is not anything serious yet. Mikki is very reserved and I am still trying to figure her out". "She is going places, she is dedicated to teaching children, very independent, very strong willed and very spoiled". "Although she is one of 6 children, her parents surrounded her with the best things, a lot of love and they told her not to settle for less". "I am starting to doubt whether or not she will stay with me".

Zavier looked over at Chris and shook his head. "Chris, I think the boy is in l-o-v-e!"

Chris patted Zavier on the back and said, "I knew it when he brought her to my mom's house!" " I knew it when he introduced her to my dad's side of the family". "He tried to convince us that he had brought other women around our family and we know that not to be true, he may have taken girls to meet his mother but, my mother and Jackson?" "You must be crazy!"

James just put down his head and did not say a word, he was going have to block out what Zavier and Chris said about him for now. But he knew in his heart that he really liked Mikki a lot. He still wasn't sure that it was love.

Mike came over and told the guys that the ladies should be back soon and wondering about dinner so they had better finish their beers and get ready because Janice had set up dinner for everyone at her cabin.

When they got to dinner, James was surprised that Janice had pulled dinner off like she did. He thought they were just going to have some take out and hang around in her cabin, but she had ordered out and did not miss a beat. She had barbecued shrimp, 2 bushels of crabs, steak, chicken, grilled vegetables, potato salad, Caesar salad and assorted fruit trays.

Janice had told everyone to dress casual and to make sure that they prepared to play all of the games they were used to. She had backgammon, she had pinochle cards, she had cards for spades, she had twister, she had a couple of mixed tapes with old school rap and they planned on party the night away.

Mikki had been quiet on her way over to Janice's cabin but James was not worried that anything was wrong because if it was she would have definitely told him about it. After they stuffed themselves with food, Gina and Mike decided that they would sneak back to the cabin that they shared with Mikki and James instead of playing spades.

Mikki sat around with Janice and a few of the other ladies while they played pinochle and laughed their heads off. Later that evening,

James and Mikki said goodnight to everyone else and made their way to the cabin.

"Did you enjoy yourself tonight James?"

"Yes, and I owe a lot of my enjoyment to you".

"You're welcome", Mikki answered.

The two of them stopped on the porch of their cabin and just gazed at the stars. James pulled Mikki to him and put his arm around her waist.

"Mikki, I'm glad that you are here to share this with me". "I want you to know that you have a special place in my heart for putting together this whole weekend for me". "I have never been with anyone who did special things like this for me".

Mikki frowned, "what do you mean by that James?

"It's hard to explain Mikki, most girls that I have dated in the past dated me for popularity because I was a Kappa and they wanted to be seen on campus, other girls have dated me because they knew that I had a car, went to college and had my own apartment and they saw me as a way of getting away from their parents and other females just wanted to be with me because I was attractive younger man to stroke their bruised egos". "Mik, you get me". "Your feathers don't get rustled at how sarcastic I can be, you can hang out and chill with me and my boys and watch sports and not complain". "I like you a lot Mikki and I know that we agreed to taking this dating thing slow, but I know in my heart that I want to see where our relationship ends up going because, I don't have to change my moods with you I can just be me".

"James, I'm glad that we had this conversation. I do enjoy spending time with you and I also want to see where this relationship ends up". "I also have to let you know that I held off on dating you because, I needed time to experience Mikki by herself and not being Kevin's girlfriend". "For years, I had been attached to him although he went to St. Joe's and I went to school in Pittsburgh". "Most of my social circle was intertwined with his and I did not want to make the mistake of rushing into another relationship". "I'm glad that we are together and I am up for whatever comes down the pike".

Suddenly the door opened and Mike stepped through. "Yo, James, your mom called and she wants you to call back as soon as possible".

James frowned and followed Mike into the cabin and sat next to the phone.

"Did she say what was wrong?" Mikki asked.

"No, as far as I know she didn't", Mike answered. "Gina answered the phone and after she got off the phone with your mom she called over to Janice's cabin to see if you two were still there and when

106

Janice told Gina that you two had left, that's when I came looking for you".

"James call her back and find out what's wrong", Mikki prodded.

For a minute, James did not move from where he was standing remembering the conversation that he had with his mother before the night before.

"Excuse me, I am going to go in the bedroom and call her and I'll be back".

Mikki, Gina and Mike just looked at each other and shrugged.

"Well, so I can give him some privacy, I guess I will just sit out here and watch TV for a while".

Mike looked at Gina and they returned to their bedroom which was down the hall. After about 5 minutes, James came out of the bedroom and sat next to Mikki and they watched TV until they fell asleep.

Mikki

Mikki got out of the shower and grabbed her housecoat and pulled off the shower cap that she had on her head. James was helping Scott and Steven and their two friends get ready for bed in guest bedroom in the basement. The kids were looking forward to having a good time at the museum tomorrow and going out to eat afterwards. It was 9:30 and the twins and Jason had been tucked in bed for about an hour. Just then the phone rang and Mikki prayed that it was not her mother in law begging for a ride home.

Mikki picked up the phone on the second ring, "Hello is my son there?" Mikki detected the nasty attitude in Regina's voice but took two deep breaths before answering.

"Hello, Regina, hold on for a minute, I will get him for you".

Regina sucked her teeth and mumbled something under her breath, but Mikki decided that it was not worth her time or effort to discuss respect at this late hour.

"James, telephone".

"Whoever, it is I'll have to call them back because, I'm busy".

"It's your mother!"

"Mik, tell my mom, I will call her back, I can't talk to her now".

With his answer being repeated, Mikki silently smiled inside and put the phone to her ear to repeat what James said to his mother.

"Regina, James said that he will call you back because he is actually putting the boys down to bed right now".

"Tell him to call me at work", and with her answer she hung up the phone before Mikki could answer.

A few minutes later, James came into the master bedroom and begun disrobing in order to get a shower. Mikki sat on the bench in front of their bed putting on lotion and wrapping her head in her sleep bonnet. As he walked down the hall to turn on the shower, Mikki reminded him that his mother called. He shook his head and grabbed his robe out of his closet and went into the bathroom to take a shower.

When he finished his shower, James toweled off and put on his pajama bottoms and grabbed the Sunday inquirer travel section and began reading. Mikki was on her side of the bed re-reading a Brenda Jackson novel and watched him silently. After a few minutes, she looked up from her book and asked him if he planned on calling his mother back. He shook his head no and told her that whatever his mother wanted it could wait, especially because she was at work tonight and he was ready to go to bed.

The next morning the phone was what woke them up instead of the kids. Mikki reached for the phone and noticed that it was only 6:30. *Who on earth would be calling us this early?*

"Hello, hold on!"

Mikki reached over and slapped James with the phone.

"Hello, yes, mom, why are you calling the house this early?" "Yes, I know you called last night and I did not call you back because, you were at work". "No, I was not going to stop my time with the kids to answer the phone". "Now that you have my attention, what is it that is so important that you have to call my house at 6:30 in the morning to wake up my family?" "What! Mom, I love you but you have got to be out of your mind!" " There is no way that I will tolerate, the disrespectful allegations that you are spewing about my wife". "How dare you!" "So what!" "You are my mother, but Mikki is my wife and I told you before that I would not tolerate that from you". "I almost lost my wife before because you wanted to be first in my life, there is no way, I'm not going to let it happen again".

By this time in the conversation James was having, Mikki was wide awake, she had sat up in bed and just listened to the intense conversation that James was having and from her point of view it was basically one sided because she had no clue as to what her mother in law was saying on the other end.

After a few minutes of James loudly speaking to his mother on the phone, Mikki had to get up and gather up the small audience that was gathering outside her master bedroom door. First Skylar came down the hall and with wide eyes watched as her father ranted and raved and yelled into the phone. Next Shannon came down the hall with Jason and his blankie in tow.

"Come on children, let's go downstairs and start breakfast, so that we can be nice and full before we leave to go to the museum".

Mikki shut the door to her bedroom and corralled the 3 children downstairs into the kitchen. She put on coffee for her and James and started the batter for pancakes and took out the turkey bacon and sausage and began cooking. Although the museum did not open until 11 am on Saturdays, Mikki figured that maybe she could keep the children occupied and out of James' way for a while until he calmed down.

About 20 minutes after she brought the children downstairs, she heard the phone crash into an upstairs wall in their master suite. She knew that James was beyond furious. James was madder than the day that he had been served with separation papers. Mikki could hear James upstairs pacing back and forth in their sitting room cursing and fussing at no one in particular.

Just then the basement door opened and Scott and Sean and their two friends Bobbie and Derek were standing there in pajamas ready to eat. Mikki needed to come up with a plan for James to calm down before the children saw him. She did not want the kids to interact with him when he was in this state of mind.

"All right kids, sit down and we will have breakfast and get dressed and I need to go to the supermarket and I will take you guys with me".

"Where's daddy", Scott asked?

"Your daddy is upstairs and before we go on our little trip to the Garden State Discovery Museum, we need to buy some more snacks to make sure you guys can hold out until we go out to the Chinese Buffet".

"Okay, Mommy".

Mikki got all of the kids settled in the kitchen eating breakfast and ran back upstairs to see that James was sitting on the chaise lounge in their sitting room fuming. She went to her closet and pulled out her clothes for this morning and proceeded to quickly jump in the shower and get dressed. When she was getting out of the shower, she heard the phone ring again.

"Hello, James answered. Mikki opened the bathroom door and asked if the phone was for her and he answered no. He shut the door to his office that was adjoined to their bedroom and shut the door. Mikki got dressed and went downstairs to find all of the kids watching television in the family room.

"Okay, guys, let's all start getting ready for our little trip to the supermarket".

Mikki escorted all of the children to their respective rooms and started delegating who was going to get in the shower first and helping the girls pick out clothes for today. After getting all of the kids dressed, Mikki told them to have a seat in the family room while she tidied up the kitchen.

Although the events of this morning were only about an hour, all of the tensions made the time pass like years. The door bell rung and Mikki was confused as to who it could be because she knew that they were not expecting anyone. Mikki answered the door and was surprised to see James' uncle John.

"Hey, Unc, how are you? What are you doing here?"

"Well, I got a call from James and he asked me to come over. Mikki, he sounded a little upset, are you guys still having trouble?"

"No, John, we are working on our marriage and we have an appointment to see a counselor on Monday. The counselor is someone at Penn counseling center that my father recommended. James and I had plans with the kids today but he got a phone call that upset him and he hasn't discussed the phone call with me".

"Okay, Mikki, I'll get to the bottom of this. Where is he?"

"He's upstairs in his office. You go and talk to him and I will take the kids to the store for some things for our trip. Come on kids, grab your jackets and so we can go to Super fresh for some snacks".

Mikki ushered the children into the garage and loaded up James' Sequoia and headed to the supermarket.

"James, yo man where you at?"

John was James' father Jackson's brother who James felt a lot more comfortable talking to. John was 9 years older than James and he was married and had 4 children ranging in age from 9 to 17. John and his wife had been college sweethearts and married soon after they both graduated from Morgan state university with degrees in accounting and business administration. James always looked to his uncle for guidance with his marriage with Mikki and he always tended to give him good straight forward advice.

John walked into the bedroom and then into the adjoining office to see James sitting in his desk looking out of the front window.

"Yo, man, you did not answer me, wassup?" " I was on my way to go and see Chris and Charmaine and then I got that frantic call from you and thought that you and Mikki were having problems again".

James looked at his uncle but still did not answer.

"James, what the hell is wrong with you man!"

James looked at his uncle and blew out a coarse sigh. "Hey Unc, it's my mom". "She just called me this morning and lambasted me for not picking her up from work last night". "She called me all kind of names and she said that Mikki was going to be the demise of me". "She basically gave me an ultimatum about where I stand with her". "You know Unc, it is hard trying to be a good son to your mother and a good husband".

"It seems like Mikki wants things from me and I try to make her happy and my mom wants things from me and I try to keep her happy as well". "I always get caught in the middle". "I love both of them and they keep putting me in the middle". "My mom always reminds me that she is my family and hints at always wanting to be first, ahead of my wife and children and Mikki is adamant that she and the kids should come first"

"But what about me, does anyone want to know what I feel?" " I feel stressed out, depressed and on edge because Mikki has already served me with separation papers and has threatened divorce and as soon as that happened my mother was there with negative words and I told you so's".

"My mom does not interact with my children, does not interact with them like a grandmother does because she is so busy raising her children and my sister's children that she does not want to be bothered with my kids". "My mother asks me to do all the things that her husband who lives there should do and finds nothing wrong with it".

"My mother has always talked negatively about Mikki to my sister and often to me but smiles in her face like everything is fine". "When Mikki got her Benz, my mother made comments about her being a spoiled brat, when we moved into this house, my mother wanted to know why we moved out of the city and that our old house was perfectly fine and Mikki only picked the house because she wanted to move me away from the family".

"Mikki has never done anything wrong to my mother or my sister". "When they have called her a bitch on the phone she has ignored them". "Before we had children, she would baby sit Sierra and Diamond and help my sister with getting them school clothes and such". "Mikki has done nothing wrong to them but they still want to trash her".

After listening and shaking his head for what seem like forever, John looked James straight in the eye and gave him an answer.

"James, you are my nephew but we grew up more like brothers because we were so close in age, but all of us saw this coming for a long time and now you are being blind sighted with it". "Your mother instilled in you a lot of things about running a household and being the man of the house, but now it appears that she is jealous of your wife".

"Mikki loves you and I know she loves you with all of your heart, and she cannot stand being, or for that matter, you allowing your mother to affect your household". "And that is what she has been trying to do for years". "Your mother may be married to Russell and he may be the father of her children, but he is not the man of the house that you were when you lived there".

"When you were a teenager, you went to school, made sure your sister got to school and when you guys got home from school, you made sure that the house was cleaned, dinner was ready and nothing was out of line". "If your mother had to work on a Saturday, you did the grocery shopping, balanced the check book; you paid bills and also had a teen age social life".

"Not all young men can do that and you grew up and found a wife that respected you for the help that you give your mother, but when you and Mikki got married, it should have been all about you two".

"Just think, when you were dating, Mikki loved you enough to be willing to compromise and work your dating schedule around things that you had to do for your mother". "Hell, I think that part of her appreciated that a man respected his mother that way".

"But getting married it should be different". "Not meaning that you have to change and stop doing things for your mother, but your priorities change". "Mikki should have been the center of that world". "She should not have had to compromise for your mother".

"Mikki noticed a long time ago, that your mother took advantage of you, but how would you have taken it if Mikki had said that to you?"

James shook his head and sighed.

"You wouldn't stand for anyone to talk badly about your mother and I think deep down that before Mikki realized that your relationship with your mother was a little flawed, you realized but you were in too deep to even know how to get out of it".

"Let's think about it, from Mikki's point of view, starting with the scripture that the pastor read at your wedding about when a man gets married how he is to uncleave from his parents and cleave to his wife because the two becomes one". "That means that your priorities change, man".

" Mikki should have been the priority and she stuck in there for a while and did not complain because both of you have stressful careers and she could understand, but where she did get fed up is when you guys started having children and the children did not become the first priority before your mother".

"I never put anything that my mother had to do before anything that the kids needed or wanted", James shouted.

"No, but you always had to compromise your time". "Best example, I can give you is when the twins had their first birthday party and you were sent to pick up their birthday cake, your mom called and wanted you to take her to get her medicine from CVS and you almost did not get the cake because the bakery was about to close because not only did you go to CVS, she made you take her to Target and the dollar store before taking her home".

"And she never even showed up at the birthday party, claiming she was too tired after work that day", James finished.

"What about the time when Mikki was pregnant with Steven and you guys went shopping at Value City with your mother and sister and they got upset when you and Mikki left and went next door to get something to eat?" "Your mother felt that it was inconsiderate of you to have her stand out in the rain?" " Anyone who has ever shopped at Value City in Springfield knows that she could have stood inside and saw when you guys went back to the car".

"And she had the audacity to complain that I put Mikki before her and that I told her that I would never put a girlfriend in front of her because she was my mother!"

"And Mikki was not my girlfriend then, she was my wife!"

" What I am trying to tell you nephew is that you really need to get your mother in check when it comes to how she interferes with your life, because if you don't Mikki is not going to give you an ultimatum, she will be gone and take that job in Atlanta that she was offered".

"What job in Atlanta- I didn't know about a job in Atlanta?"

"Look nephew, you know that Mikki was upset that she gave you that ultimatum and from your actions in the past concerning your mother, she sent out her resume to Atlanta and she had some very interested employers". "I know that she applied to jobs in Atlanta because she was discussing it with Janice when we came over to visit her when you guys were separated".

"Oh", James said. "She would have taken my children with her? I need to really sit down and think about all that has happened, but right now I need to get dressed and spend the day with my children and wife to show them how important they are to me". "Unc, thank you for stopping by, but I need to make up for all of my past transgressions and work on fighting to keep my marriage intact".

James walked his uncle downstairs and locked the door behind him and ran upstairs to get dressed for a day full of fun with his family.

Mikki unloaded the children from James' truck and gave the older ones permission to go in the back yard and play on the swings. Mikki helped Shannon and Skylar out of the car and picked up Jason and went into the house. Once she opened the door of the mud room, James was right there to take Jason out of her arms.

"Thanks, I'll get the bags out of the car". "Shannon and Skylar go in the family room and watch cartoons until we get ready to leave". Mikki went back out to the car and began unloading the bags.

As soon as she turned around she ran directly into James who was trying to reach for some of the bags.

"So, did you have a good conversation with John?"

"Yes and he gave me a lot of insight on my problem".

"Oh, I hope it works out for you". Mikki did not like that James was being secretive with her; she could always count on James to be open and honest with her about everything.

James shut the backdoor to the car and they both went into the house and placed all of the bags on the counter and began unloading.

"So Mikki, when were you going to tell me about Atlanta?"

Mikki looked up from her bag with a shocked look on her face.

"Uh, how did you find out about Atlanta? John?" " James, just understand that, I did that because I was upset with you and I haven't pursued it any further". "I made a rash decision and I know that it would have been hurtful and after, I calmed down I had a clear head and decided against it". "I would never deliberately move the children away from you and not allow you to see them". "I know you love them with all of your heart, I'm not that cold hearted".

James came over to Mikki and wrapped his arms around her waist. "Mik, I love you and I want you to know that". "I made a promise when you said that I could come back home, to work on building this relationship to be a strong foundation of love and trust". "I know that you would not have let me come back home if you did not believe me and I am not concerned about the Atlanta thing". "Finding out about Atlanta, made me deal with a lot of things that I don't think I really have ever put fully into perspective and I need to start doing that now". "We won't talk anymore about what's going to happen, but I plan on showing you". "Now with all of that said, let's get this food put away, our snacks packed and let's take our children out to have a fun day with their parents!"

The day had been a fun one. Mikki, Skylar and Shannon were in her car and James, Jason, Scott and his friend Bobbie and Steven and his friend Derrick were in James' truck. When they arrived home at 7, Mikki took the little ones and put them to bed while James helped the Bobbie and Derrick pack up their bags so that he could drop them off at their respective homes.

Just then the phone rang and Mikki ran over to the desk in the kitchen to answer it. "Hello?"

"Can you tell James to get on the phone?" " I need to talk to him".

Mikki frowned and looked at the phone knowing that it was her mother in law and she did not sound pleasant.

"Regina, he's on his way out can I have him call you back".

"No, bitch, I'll call him on his cell phone". Click!

Mikki looked at the phone and was fuming. "I don't believe that she called me a bitch!" " I would be in my right mind to call her back and cuss her out!"

"Cuss who out?" Mikki jumped and turned around to see James standing behind her in the kitchen.

"Where did you come from? I thought you were driving the Bobbie and Derrick home?"

"We were in the garage and I had to come back because, I picked up your keys and not mine?" " Oh? So who are you going to cuss out?"

"That was your mother on the phone- Before Mikki could finish, the cell phone that James wore on his hip rang.

"And that may be her now", Mikki finished.

James took his phone out of the clip and looked at the caller id and flipped his phone open. "Hello, yes, I need to call you back, I can't talk right now and he hung up".

James went over to Mikki, "what did she say to you babe?" "Tell me Mikki!"

Mikki looked at James before answering. "James, your mother called me a bitch, and I am really tiring of the thought that she cannot call here and speak to me respectfully on the phone". "I don't know what you have been telling her about our separation, but her calling here has gotten worse than it was before our separation". "At least before our separation, I could deal with the rude way she talked to me on the phone, but she blatantly called me a bitch! I cannot take much more of this!"

James put his hands on Mikki's shoulder forcing her to look directly at him. "Babe, I don't know what my mom's problem is but I will address it and if need be I will change our house phone number and my cell phone number is she cannot be respectful". "I don't want my children to be privy to that kind of action and you don't deserve nor have to put up with that kind of nonsense".

"Mik, please understand that I still want to keep our appointment with the counselor next week so that we can talk to a professional about all of the things going on between us as well as the new developments from this morning with my mom. I'll sit down and tell you about this morning and the insight that I got from my uncle John".

Mikki lowered her head in thought.

"Mik, we are going to make it through this, I know it"

"I know you will work hard James, but I do not want to talk anymore about your mom. We have guests coming tomorrow and I just want to get ready for tomorrow and I promise that when all our guests are gone, we will sit down and talk about this".

James shook his head and walked out the kitchen.

Mikki made her way to the front door to see who was standing on her front porch.

"Hey girl, long time no see!"

"Hey Mike, glad to see you and boy don't you sound country!"

"Now don't you be getting all sassy with my husband miss thang!"

Hugs went all around for Mike, Gina and MJ and Mikki ushered them inside.

"Oh! Mikki, the house is so nice; I see you guys have been working on making it your home in the last year".

" Yes, girl, you know it takes time when you get in a new home but eventually you get to where you want to be and its comfortable".

"Yo, frat! Where you at?"

Just then Scott, Steven and Jason came running up the basement stairs and grabbed Mike.

"Hey little guys, how have you been? I haven't seen you guys in a while".

"Uncle Mike, where's MJ and did you bring us something from North Carolina? The boys said in unison.

"Yes, Uncle Mike brought you something, I brought you all some Tar Heel t-shirts and caps".

"Yeah! The boys all shouted!"

"MJ, come on down stairs so we can show you our play station!"

MJ took off with the boys to the basement.

"Hey, Mike, Gina how are you two doing?" James came out of the kitchen and hugged Gina and gave Mike a hand shake. "My wife here has been telling me that you guys will be relocating to Owings Mills?"

"Yes sir, so we can be closer to our family as well as good friends".

The door bell rang and Mikki turned to go answer it.

"It's Zavier, Leslie and Tim and Michelle".

"Hey", they all shouted as Mikki opened the door.

Michelle ran over to Gina and said hello and Tim and Zavier went over to speak with James and Mike. The course of the day went well when and the friends sat back and enjoyed watching their children play together and the adults playing cards, catching up on old times and laughing.

Just then the phone rang and Leslie picked it up and answered, "Steven's residence".

"Tell James to get the phone!"

"Excuse me, who may I ask is calling?"

"Don't worry about it bitch! Just tell James to get the phone".

Leslie walked over to where James was laughing with Tim, Mike, Zavier, Chris, John and his neighbor Allen.

"Who is it for Leslie?

"It's for you but the person on the other end definitely does not have any manners!"

James took the phone from his sister-in law and frowned. "Hello? What is the matter with you Rita? Why can't you call my house and have some respect?"

James walked away from the eyes that were watching him and listening to his one sided conversation. James went into the guest bedroom and shut the door so that he could continue his conversation.

"Look Rita, I understand what mom told you about our discussion, but you have nothing to do with this. Mom wants me to be more to her than I can be right now and I have to worry about losing my family. I can't be around or talk to mom for awhile, at least until I have a handle on what Mikki and I are going to do".

"No, we are not talking divorce but, I owe it to my kids and Mikki to try and work things out here first before I go and stroke mom's ego". "Well, I am glad that you and your new boyfriend are working out and I will definitely talk to you soon"

James hung up the phone and for once he was glad that his sister did not immediately take his mother's side this time. Rita still did not get along with Mikki but since she got her own apartment and her and the girls were not under the same roof their mother and her father Russell, Rita seemed to be doing a lot better. James opened the guest room door and went back to talk with his friends.

Mikki saw James go into the guest room when he got that call and wondered who he was actually speaking to. Ever since, he and his mom had that major blow out the day before she felt like anything would just make him blow his top, so she always advised the kids to be extra quiet and she just tried to stay out of his way.

"Mikki, here comes Tasha, Kevin, and the kids and boy does Tasha look big! Leslie elbowed her and pointed in their direction as they walked up the drive way.

Gina ran down the steps of the deck and walked over to Tasha and gave her a hug. Kevin and his teenage son Jamal walked over to where the men were and started shaking hands all around.

The rest of the evening progressed without incident and everyone enjoyed themselves.

Later, Mikki walked Mike and Gina to the car and hug and promised each other that they would call each other more often. James and Mikki walked up the driveway with their arms around each other smiled.

"James, I'm glad that we had everyone over tonight".

"So, am I Mik. It was good to have our friends and our family and children over just hanging out without any stress".

"Well, I guess we should get ready for tomorrow, our appointment is at 10 and we have to drop the kids off before we head into the city". Mikki, dropped her arm from around James waist and started to head up the stairs to go to bed, but James grabbed her and pulled her back to him and gave her a kiss on the cheek and hugged her deeply.

"Mikki, I want you to know that I love you and I am going to work hard for us". Before Mikki could answer him he kissed her deeply on the lips and pulled her closer to him. Once he released her, she just stared at him and shook her head because she was so touched by the gesture that she was speechless.

The next morning after the kids were dropped off, Mikki and James rode silently on I-95 into the University City section for their appointment at Penn Center. James immediately found a spot and pulled in. They both took deep breaths and grabbed what they needed and went in.

When they got in the center, they met the receptionist and gave her the information for their appointment and she gave them some paperwork to fill out and have a seat. Not knowing actually what to expect, Mikki was pleasantly surprised at the décor and the whole feel of the office. The waiting room was decorated with sage green walls, accented with beiges, mauves and some hunter green.

There were some couches and some chairs and over in one corner there was an ample magazine rack with various titles and a television which was currently playing NBC 10's morning show 10!. Mikki walked over to the rack while James finished filling out the paper work and picked up a parenting magazine and started leafing through it. James returned the paperwork and paid the fee for their initial counseling session.

After about 20 minutes, they were called back to initially begin their meeting.

"Hello, Mr. and Mrs. Stevens, my name is Janice Stein and I am the intake social worker here, before you two meet with a psychologist, I am going to get some background information so that our staff will have the full picture of how we can actually help you two".

After talking to the both of them, Janice decided to give them information on the Intimate Relationship Skills program and the Relationship Enhancement Program but also how to go about setting up individual marriage counseling and individual counseling with the group.

She then advised them that they would both have individual sessions today so that once they were assigned to any of the programs that they offered; they would be able to address both of their concerns.

After sitting with Janice for 45 minutes, they were both assigned to two different social workers so that they could address their personal concerns. By the end of their 2 hour session, they had information on what they needed and an appointment at the Concordville office for their first joint session. They walked out to the car and they both were quiet. Mikki thought to herself that she really wanted this to work and god help them if it didn't.

After spending half their day with social workers and psychologists, James was exhausted. He went into his office and closed the door and turned on his laptop to check his messages at work. He saw that his mailbox was full and he decided that he would look at his email when his cell phone rang.

"Good afternoon, James Stevens speaking".

"James this is your mother and I would really appreciate it if you would come over to my house so that we could talk".

"I'm doing fine mom, my day is going well and you?"

"Son, spare me all of the technicalities, I need to talk to you today and I have been keeping my distance, but I need to talk to you about our situation and how your wife is making you stay away from your family and not help us".

"Mom, have you ever thought that maybe your actions against my wife have made me not want to deal with you?"

"Are you crazy son, I am your mother, and when that wife of yours decides that you are no longer good enough for her, who is going to have your back?"

"Mom, do you honestly think that you have had my back? You look out for yourself and make sure that you are okay, especially because your husband does not do what he is supposed to do? You know what, let's stop this conversation before, I say something that is disrespectful and hurts your feelings. I'm tired mom, I don't have time to talk, because I have a conference call in 15 minutes and I want to make sure that I am on time for that and then I have to pick Jason up from day care when I'm done with that".

"Well, can you come in the morning to talk?"

"Does this also mean that you want a ride to work tomorrow?"

"It would be nice, it's the least you can do son?"

"Look mom, I will be there by 1 so that we can talk and then I will drop you off at work. I'll see you tomorrow".

"Bye son".

James dropped his cell phone onto the desk and looked out of the window. He sighed, "I just can't take too much of this- Mikki wants my time and my mother is demanding my time. Mikki is my wife and we have children together and a life and my mother is demanding that I be the man in her life, regardless of the fact that she has a husband that is extremely capable. What is a good brother like me to do?"

James looked at his watch and he picked up the office phone and called the 800 number that he needed to call so that he could participate in his conference call with his boss and team members.

The door to Mikki's office opened and she watched as Gina strolled in. "Well good afternoon, to you Mrs. Stevens, so how did everything go?"

Gina looked good as always, she had on a pink Nike track pants with green Philadelphia Eagles t-shirt and a pink Eagles cap. Her shoulder length hair was pulled back into a ponytail that was secured at the nape of her neck with a small gold barrette. She was not showing yet but she had the glow of motherhood.

"Well, we met with a social worker and a psychologist and we have an appointment set up in two weeks at the Concordville office". "Gina, I really hope that this all works out, I mean, the Atlanta recruiter emails me once a month with jobs in their school systems down there and because I am certified as a site director and I also have my master's in special education, she keeps reminding me that I will easily get a job that will pay the moving costs for me and the family".

"But there is no way that I am going to run from my problems". "I know that James loves me and the children, but his mom has him by the balls". "She believes that he should always be her savior and run to her aid when she calls".

"Look, Mik, I am your girl and I have been there for you as you were going through all of this". "I told you a long time ago, that James' family always took your kindness for weakness and because you were always willing to compromise so that they could be happy, you gave James the easy way out". "He needs to make this decision and put his foot down and address it".

"Gina, he doesn't see it that way, he always says that I should be woman enough to sit down and have a conversation with his mother about the way that I feel, but I don't necessarily think that it is between the both of us". "I think that it is for him to do".

"Mik, I agree, but you can't compromise anymore".

"Oh, Gina, I haven't but when, I don't compromise, it makes an argument between me and James and we are back to square one again". "I tell James constantly that, when his family demands his time like that, it affects the whole family, not just him". "He can't continue to try and balance two families at once".

"Mik, I want you to try and work things out, now that you are going to counseling, I really would not like you to up and move to Atlanta and split the children from their father or for you to move away from Mike, MJ, me and the new baby now that we are moving back to the area".

"I know, Gina, it would suck now that you are back in the area and I decide to get out of dodge and my marriage".

Gina walked over to Mikki and gave her a hug. "Don't worry honey, it will work out, I promise, now let's go". "I want to treat you to lunch and also do a little shopping for the new nursery". "We can head over Macy's in Springfield to see if they are having a sale".

Mikki walked over to her closet and grabbed her purse and blazer and walked out of her office door behind Gina.

"James, would you please come on, we have to meet my parents and my grandparents for dinner". "We need to leave now, so that we will be able to get a good parking spot!".

Mikki was dressed nicely in black merino wool slacks, with a red cashmere mock neck sweater and Aigner loafers. She wore a gold Figaro link chain that carried her initial and a matching bracelet and gold hoop earrings in her ear. Her shoulder length brownish red hair was cut in a stylish layered bobb with ash blond highlights. Mikki sipped on a cup of lemon tea, because all day she felt queasy and could not keep anything down.

James came out of their bedroom and walked over to Mikki and put his arms around him. "Are you sure, you feel up to this, Mik?" "I know you haven't been able to keep anything down all day, do you really think that we should go out to dinner with everyone?"

"James, you know that we leave to go away with Gina and Mike to Cancun for the holidays and my grandmother will not let us hear the end of it, if she doesn't see us before we leave".

"I know Mik, but I worry about you, if you are sick now, what about when we get to Mexico. I want to be able to do all kinds of things to you, when we get away like I did when we were on our honeymoon".

"I know James, but I think that this is just a 24 hour bug that a lot of the students have at school". "And to think about it, you have had me all to yourself for the last six months, since we got married".

"I know, but there is a big difference when you are in a tropical location and you don't have to worry about being interrupted by the everyday things of life". "I am just surprised that Mike and Gina are going to be able to get away with a MJ being only 18 months old and convincing Mike's parents to keep him for a week so that they can have a belated honeymoon".

"Well, you know that a lot of things were rushed with them, especially when Gina found out she was pregnant with MJ, Mike was about to relocate to North Carolina for his job, so they had to get married and set up house really quickly".

"Well, Mr. Stevens, I think that we should get going, before my mother calls here to find out if we left already".

"Let me change my belt and grab my leather jacket and we can be on our way".

Mikki grabbed the gifts that they planned on exchanging with her parents and grandparents and headed toward the door. When James came out of the bedroom, they headed out the door and outside to his car. They made it to the Houlihan's in Rittenhouse square in no time. They parked in the garage across the street and headed to restaurant

As soon as they walked in, they saw Mikki's grandfather Thomas decked out in his Sunday best. For a man in his mid eighties, he was still sharp as a tack. He had on grey hounds tooth slacks, with a matching grey sweater vest, grey silk tie, a light blue dress shirt and a matching hat. James knew that the matching solid color grey blazer was probably hanging up along with his black wool overcoat.

"Hi, granddad, Mikki said as she walked over to him and hugged him.

"Hi, baby doll, how are you? Good evening James". "Baby doll, you don't look to well, what's going on?"

"I'm fine granddad, I just think that I may have caught the bug that my students are passing around". "I'm better than I was this morning, but I think that I still look a little pale".

"Well, let's go in here and get dinner started so you can have something on your stomach".

"Let's do that". James opened the door and they all walked over to where Mikki's parents and her grandmother Delores were engaged in conversation.

"Look who, I met up with in the hallway gang!"

Mikki's parents and her grandmother all looked up and said hello at the same time. They all sat down and got comfortable and started ordering appetizers and discussing the trip that James and Mikki had planned to Cancun.

When their appetizers came, Mikki had to excuse herself due to the nausea that she began to feel once the food was sat down at the table. Mikki's mother ran after her into the bathroom.

"Mikki, are you okay?"

"Yes, mom, I haven't been feeling good all day, and I think that I have come down with the bug that is going around the school".

"I'll say that you have some bug alright! I'll tell you right now what bug that is".

Mikki came out of the stall and washed her hands and wet a paper towel to look at her mother.

"And what bug is that, mom?"

"Girl you've got pregnant written all over you".

"Mom, I just think that I have a bug and it is not pregnancy".

"I'm going to tell you, a mother knows these things".

"Mom, can we please just go back and enjoy dinner, I think that I will be alright now".

"Well, I will leave you alone for now, but I want you to make sure that you go make an appointment with your doctor if this bug of yours continues for another day".

"I will mom".

The two of them went back to the table and enjoyed the rest of their dinner. They exchanged gifts and were glad that Mikki's parents and grandparents enjoyed their gifts. They all parted ways after desert and Mikki was quiet all the way home. When they got home James reminded Mikki that they needed to finish packing and get ready for their trip. Mikki just shook her head and went into their bedroom and got ready for bed.

The next morning, Mikki was pre-occupied with what her mother had said the night before and while she was in the drugstore she picked up a pregnancy test and remembered that she had a doctor's appointment that afternoon and decided she would ask the doctor to run the test before she got her vaccination for their trip. She had enough time to go and pick up her passport and pick up a few last minutes things before driving to University of Pennsylvania for her doctor's appointment.

Once she got to her doctor's appointment she was nervous, but she knew that she had to prove her mother's accusations to be wrong, there was just no way could that she be pregnant, just six months after getting married. Mikki took a look around the office and found that it was nice and soothing; decorated in beiges, cranberry and light greens. There were two ladies and one gentleman at the check in desk and there was a lot of cherry wood. In one area of the waiting room was a play area for children which was decorated in bright colors, there were coloring books and toys and a television playing Disney movies.

In the other section of the room the television was playing The View and Mikki could not help and say to herself how much the young girl Debbie got on her nerves. She had checked in, she was just waiting for someone to call her back into the room. She liked her doctor; one thing about Dr. Harris was that she was straight forward.

Mikki found out about Dr. Harris from Tasha who worked for her when Mikki volunteered to watch her god-daughter Kayla. Kayla had gotten sick and when Mikki called Kevin, he directed her to take her to Tasha's job and Dr. Harris would see her.   A few minutes later, Dr. Harris came out and called Mikki back into the exam room.

"Hey, Dr. Harris, since when do you start bringing your own patients back to exam rooms?"

"Since we are so backed up because one of the Medical Assistants is at lunch and Tasha is helping Dr. Anderson with a procedure".

Mikki walked into the exam room and put her purse and jacket down on the chair and hopped onto the exam table.

"So, I hear that you are going away with that new handsome husband of yours for the holidays?"

"Yes, we are going away with our friends Mike and Gina, this is like a belated honeymoon for them and just some time for the 4 of us to hang out together".

"Dr. Harris, I need to take a pregnancy test while I'm here today. I have been not able to keep food down for a few days this week. I thought maybe that I had some type of bug that had been going around at the school but my mother tends to think otherwise".

"Well, that may be something we need to check into before giving you this vaccination for your trip". "I would be a little wary about giving you a vaccination if you were pregnant". "Let me get a urine sample and I will get one of the phlebotomist to come in and draw some blood". "If the urine sample is positive, we may have to hold off on giving you that shot before you go away".

Mikki said, "Okay", but then frowned. Later that day, she had confirmation on what her mother said and she had to go home and tell James the news.

When James walked into the house, he heard the sounds of children laughing and a Cinderella movie playing. He hung his coat and walked into the bedroom and found Mikki and her three nieces, Tanya, Tamara and Tia lying on their stomachs watching the movie.

Tia turned around and squealed, "Uncle James, I have been waiting for you!"

Mikki turned around and lipped hello to him and the other two ran over and jumped on him as well.

"Hey, Honey, I brought some Jerk Chicken from the Jamaican Jerk Hut and some plantains, the girls already ate because they wanted stuff from Wendy's and you know, I am just a sucker for the puppy dog faces".

James did not bother to even look up, because he was playing with Tia, throwing her up in the air and tickling her. Mikki just smiled and figured she would tell him the news once her sister came to pick up the girls.

The rest of the night went quite smoothly, with James and Mikki entertaining the girls and watching movies. By the time her sister arrived, the girls were asleep and in their pajamas and Mikki was just finishing up putting their last bit of stuff into suitcases.

Leslie came back in the house to pick up the girls back pack and to hug her sister.

"Mikki, are you alright? You look a little pale?"

"I'm okay, but I just have to let you know that after all these years of you being a mommy, you are going to be an auntie!"

Leslie grabbed her sister and hugger her tightly. "Well, what did James say?"

"What did James say about what?"

Leslie and Mikki turned around to see that James had walked into the living room and overheard part of the conversation.

"James, you know that I went to doctors this morning to get my shot for our trip?"

James shook his head and watched as his sister in law slipped out of the apartment door.

"Well, James, I just found out that I am about 6 weeks pregnant and that is why I had been feeling sick lately. I have already made an appointment with the OB/GYN for the first week of January".

"James picked up Mikki and started jumping around with her. I am so excited babe! That will make my Christmas gift, so much more exciting".

Mikki looked at James and knew that he was sincere in his excitement.

"So what is your Christmas gift, I thought that our trip was the Christmas gift because we are saving so that we can buy a house", Mikki asked.

"Well, I just wanted to make you believe that our trip was the only thing that we were going to do for Christmas because, I think that I found our dream house and if we are having a baby, I want to take you to see it and get your approval because, I really believe that we can swing it because the mortgage may not be more than what we pay for our apartment to rent".

"So how about we go and drive by the house before we go check into the hotel for our flight tomorrow?"

"Are you serious James? You found us a house?"

"No, I stumbled across the house and I have the realtor's card and we can make an appointment to see the house and then go from there".

"Mikki, I would not make a decision about a house without your support, you know that right?" James grabbed Mikki by the waist and pulled her close, "anything that I decide to do that concerns us, will not go ahead without your approval. You can best believe that!"

Mikki kissed James on his cheek and shook her head. "James, I know that we are going to work at making this marriage succeed in every way possible. So, I can't and I won't doubt you. But if I don't like the house, I will say no. And then we will talk with the realtor about helping us find a house that will suit us and the new addition".

"So hurry and go get your jacket so you can show me this house before we go to check in at the Sheraton".

"You know what Mik? I love you"

"And I love you. Now get moving!"

James

James was in the waiting room nervous about his first session with the counselor. He knew that he had to take this by the bulls and run with it, in order to make his wife happy and in order for his family to be back together. He had arrived almost an hour early with his lap top and his cell phone , just in case he needed to be contacted while away from the office but he knew that once he went into his session he would have to turn all of that off.

The last couple of weeks had been trying for him at best. He knew that Mikki attitude toward him was improving, but she walked on eggshells because she just did not know what was going to go awry and she could not let herself lose control again.

He thought to himself, that in some ways Mikki was being unreasonable, but he knew that his mother and her demands had put Mikki on the defense and she was going to go all out to protect her and the kids.

"James, Good afternoon, my name is Brenda Ratcliff and I will be your counselor during this session. Come on back into my office".

James reached down and turned off his cell phone and followed her into her office.

"Have a seat James. Let me just explain to you what we try and accomplish during these individual sessions". "We begin by letting you get off your chest your frustrations, expectations, etc on why you are here and then give you an idea of how we can assist you with achieving the goals that you set for yourself".

"Excuse me Brenda, but I am here to save my marriage, I know that there is no little pill that will cure what is going on, but from what I understand, you are telling me that the whole success of this lies with me and my wife?"

"Yes, James, we as counselors at this center, we only listen and evaluate and assist you with listening- meaning really understand what the other in your relationship has been saying to you".

"It is obvious that you are having some miscommunication issues and they are not being resolved".

"Okay, so you are saying that you just plan on being a mediator in this whole thing?" "My wife and I communicate fine". "We discuss everything under the sun".

"But James, if you both understand what it is that each other is really saying or what the other one is really feeling, then you would not be here at all".

"Touché, Brenda. I think I can be receptive to all that is going to be put to me today and work on it. I have to; I can't lose my wife and children. I don't think that I would be anything without them".

"On that note, I think that is where we begin this session by you giving me some of your background on just you". "Let's just make this a background session on you and how you grew up, so that I can understand how early relationships may or may not have affected the way you relate to your wife"

"Okay, well where do I start?"

"Anywhere you want, but I will help you understand how early relationships with anyone important in your life, stay with you throughout your life and ultimately affect any relationship that you may have".

"I am the oldest son of my mother, who never married my father, because he was forced to marry my step-mother. Until a year before my sister was born, it was pretty much my mother and I. I had visitation with my father and was welcomed into his new family with open arms".

"I know that during the times that I was away from my mother which was almost every weekend, she was always happy to see me when I came back". "My mother was a young mother, she had me at the age of 16 and because her aunt who was the guardian of her at the time did not like that she got pregnant, my mother was given 6 months' rent and told that she would have to make it on her own because she could not live with her aunt anymore".

"My mom, did well, she went to school at night and worked during the day so that she graduated high school at 17 and went to Community College to take classes to become an Administrative Assistant. She got a job at Pennsylvania Hospital as a clerk and she has been there ever since".

"When I was about 4, she met her current husband and my sister and 2 brother's father, Russell. They did not get married until 9 years later approximately six months before my mother gave birth to my brother Russell Jr".

"Because there is 8 years between my sister and I and because for a long time before my mother married Russell; I was still responsible at home. By the time my sister was born, I was able to go food shopping with the money that my mother left at home as well as be responsible for depositing money in the bank for my mother or taking her paycheck and whatever cash Russell gave her and write checks to pay bills".

"James, don't you think that is a little strange for an 8 year old boy to be doing? I mean, your mother was involved with a man and she was putting the responsibility to run a household on you".

"You weren't the man of the house, this was time when you should have been playing with toys and being a child".

"I had a childhood, I still did typical boy things like play with my friends, go to summer camp but I did not do things with my friends until, I made sure that what my mother left for me to do was taken care of".

Brenda just shook her head.

James continued. "By the time, I was 14, I would go to school, go to football practice, pick up my sister and brothers from day care, come home make sure we both had dinner, check her homework, make sure that they both had a bath and by the time Russell came home, made sure that he had dinner and there was a plate put aside for my mother who often worked a little bit later than Russell".

"Because my mother had two other children after my sister, I needed to stay home to go to college because I was needed to help at home".

"I'm confused James, you were taking on the responsibility and making sacrifices like you were the husband and you were not; and your mother was married and her husband never took over the responsibility of being the man of the house?"

"Does Russell have animosity towards you? I mean does he have good things to say about you when you are around?"

"James thought about it for a minute. "Russell and I don't really have a relationship". "I mean, I always spent time with my dad and my dad was the best dad that he could have been to me but I sometimes get into shouting matches with him because I don't think he uses the best judgment when it comes to my mom and my siblings".

"How would you know if he uses the best judgment with them if you were always there to step in and your mother always deflects to you for help? Have you ever considered that as a child you were constantly put in the role of the man of the house and never stepped down from that role when Russell came on the scene?"

"Look, I want you to jot these questions down and really put yourself in Russell's shoes for a minute. He loves your mother and they have children together but the role of the provider and the one that handles everything is a boy". "Technically, I say a boy because, when your sister was born you were a child and because partly due to your mother's grooming of you at a young age she deflects to you, relies on you- but what type of relationship can her and her husband have if you are always the one to handle it?"

"Here is the best way for you to really envision what I am talking about. You and Mikki are married and the only say that you have in your marriage is to give money to Mikki, have sex with Mikki but you have no say in how she raises the kids, you can't discipline the kids and you have no say in how the money is spent, what activities the kids participate in and Mikki just does whatever she wants".

"I don't want you to answer that right now, but I want you write in the journal that I gave you and then next week when we meet, you will have your first group session with some other men who are having issues with their spouses as well and I want you to discuss your answers in that group setting and then again with me the following week".

"I'm confused, how is this going to help me with me and Mikki's situation?"

Brenda leaned up in her chair and grabbed James' hand. "Trust me, I know what I'm doing and we need to take this one step at a time. I just ask that you participate in what we tentatively have called TMBP here at the center because when we did both you and your wife's intake, we believed that you two were candidates for this groundbreaking research and counseling project and if all goes well, the information that we gather from you and Mikki as well as some of the other participants we will be able to save some lives".

"Okay, I will be open minded about this, but I need my family back and I will do anything to make sure that my family dynamic is back and fully operational and there is not divorce in mine and Mikki's future".

James walked out of therapy, thinking that he would focus on all that Brenda said to him today, but he was definitely emotionally spent from all that he told her and hoped to just go home and spend time with

Mikki and the kids. He turned on his phone and clipped his hands free device to his ear and walked to his car. Once his phone was fully booted, he saw that he had 10 missed calls. He scrolled to see that 8 of them were from his mother.

"I will call her back later; I need to get home so that I can make dinner with Mikki and the kids".

Mikki

Mikki wanted to surprise James when he got home with his favorite meal to let him know that she was glad that they were moving forward with the counseling and working to get back on track. The kids were stretched out in the family room watching cartoons on the Disney channel and were all cleaned up and ready for dinner. Mikki looked at the timer for the garlic bread and as long as James walked in the door in the next 20 minutes they were all set. Mikki tried not to be anxious about whether he went through with counseling or if he was going to be late arriving home due to a distraction from his mother. Her counselor had advised her of that when she was in her session earlier this afternoon.

"Hello, Mikki, my name is Brenda and I am the counselor working with both you and your husband. I was so excited when I got both of your cases because this will help me not only to understand mother and sons relationship, it will also help me obtain more grant money for my TMBP project".

"TMBP- what does that stand for? It's The Momma's Boy Project. I came up with that name because I was married to a man, who was the oldest son of his single mother and we had a lot of difficulties". "I was very angry about the situation and unable to deal with the ups and downs of the demands that his mother made of him. I honestly did not know what hit me once we got married because; when we were dating it was so different".

"I have been doing research on men and their mother's and I have found out that the Momma's boy syndrome as I like to call it, can be found in families where there are two parents, it is not just limited to race and the syndrome comes in different phases".

"Something that was really bothering me has turned into a research project. Some believe that men always have an Oedipus complex when it comes to their mothers but the momma boy syndrome is something different".

"In essence, you have a couple of type of different momma's boys. First, you have the ones who mom does everything for them, so when they get with a woman, they expect the same. Some of these men's have successful relationships because they either find a woman that takes over that role, or they find one who shows them that they need to learn to do simple things in order for their relationship to work and the men take on that challenge for love. These men can come from single parent homes or from two parent households".

The next types of momma's boy that I have discovered are the ones where the mother's mold the sons to be the men that they wanted in their own lives. These men typically learn at a young age to be the man of the house. Although the mother's may push them to go to school and be educated and get good jobs; the mother's believe in the long run that , I raised a man who will take care of me for always because he will appreciate the love and time that I devoted to making him the man he is today".

"We often see women who date men to do the same thing, but the in the mother son dynamic, the mother uses a lot of guilt to make the son feel guilty and continue doing things for well beyond the time that would be considered for a grown child to be helping out. Often times, it appears that the grown son is supporting the mother.

"In this case, if there are other children, whether close in age or not, the other children whether girl or boy, feel like they don't measure up and do a lot of acting out to get attention from the mother or they tend to not do anything because they become tired of trying to see attention from the mother. In this instance, if the child after the oldest son is a girl, the girl tends to act out tremendously because in a manner of speaking, the boys usually leave the nest and girls tend to take care of momma. With not having the option of taking care of momma taken away, the girl sibling has to get attention in some other way".

Also, if there is a spouse to the mother that fits into this equation, the spouse is made to feel inadequate because the mother does not confer with the spouse about decisions or money planning but the mother speaks with the child about decisions in general. Although, the mother may be in a relationship with a spouse or significant other, the mother tends to by any means necessary sabotage the son's relationships.

"Often times, it works but from my research, a lot of these men get married; and they are fully aware of the draining situation with their mother. It takes love and a strong woman to help them break the cycle. Not all of these marriages sustain and grow but I have had the opportunity to see marriages that can overcome this whole situation".

"Brenda that's a whole lot to digest. I really never considered that my situation was close to anyone else. I thought this was something new. And after hearing all that you said, I can see that James does fit the category. But I don't know if I am willing to continue to fight and be the bad guy. I just want my children to have access to their father and not have to wait or have him answer, we can do this after I make sure that Grandma is okay. I think that when we were dating, I figured, I really did not mind that we rearranged our schedules. But I refuse to compromise that for my children".

"I can understand what you are saying Mikki, however, in some instances because James is aware of the situation and could have possibly been aware that he is being used in a manner by his mother, he may not be able to adequately make the change so that this will stop. Both you and his mother are dear to him and have strong personalities but his mother has the fact that she is his mother and guilt on her side".

"Well, I guess you gave me a lot to think about. But I have to tell you that it is not all good. If, I knew back then what I know now; I may have ran for the hills and never turned back. I do have a strong personality, but I come from a family where, our parents put us first and time for each other was never compromised by my grandparents. I wouldn't say that it was all peaches and cream but I know that family was first in my father's eyes and vice versa. Suffice to say, my grandfather passed away long before I was born, and my grandmother never relied on any of her children. She may have asked for favors, but until she was diagnosed with liver cancer at the age of 86 my grandmother did a lot of things for herself".

"Well, Mikki our time is just about over, and I think you have a lot to think about; I want you to move forward with James by being open with him about your feelings as well as when voicing those opinions or feelings to him that you are calm". If you have to take a minute and come back to talk to him and ask that when you talk that he repeats back to you in your own words what you are expressing will help as well. I have James scheduled for a group session with some of the other men in my study group and I will see you next week again for a one on one to discuss whether the techniques that I gave you are working".

"So when will we move to couples counseling?"

"I currently don't think you two are ready for that yet. I think, that moving forward we will hold off on couples counseling until after James has had a few group sessions with other men like him and then we will decide on couple therapy for the both of you".

"Trust me, Mikki, I have both you and James best interest at heart. I see the worry on your face but I believe that if we take this step by step and you both work on the things that I give you; there will success. I will see you next week".

Mikki just shook her head and picked up her purse and brief case and walked out of the office. "I hope she's right about all this, I would hate to fail at my marriage and walk away thinking it was my fault.

James

James pulled up in the garage and was happy that he was at home and although his mom's number came up in the caller id about 4 times he wasn't tempted to answer it. He needed to have some carefree time with Mikki and the kids and not worry about what was going on at his mom's house. He walked in the house and could smell that Mikki had made his favorite dinner and was setting the table for all 7 of them to eat dinner at the kitchen table.

He smiled, Mikki had on his favorite color. She was wearing a red short sleeved blouse with grey hounds tooth slacks and she had changed out of her red sling back pumps that he knew she wore earlier and was walking around in her favorite flip flops. Her hair was pulled back into ponytail with a butterfly clip. She always pulled her hair up in a ponytail when she wanted to get things done.

"Hey babe, I'm home and I come bearing gifts".

Mikki turned from the table to face him and gave him a smile.

"Are those gifts for me or to bribe your children?

"No actually, I brought gifts for everyone. Yours are these hydrangeas and something else you will get later and for my children, I got passes to Oasis fun center which include power up cards with $15 worth of power coins. So, am I the best daddy and husband in the world?"

Shannon and Skylar ran to give James a big hug. The boys did not move from their spots in front of the TV but all shouted in unison, "Thanks Dad"

"James, don't you know that they still have power up cards from the last birthday party that they all went to there?"

"Honey, I know but I couldn't resist especially because, I wanted us to probably take the kids to Oasis on Saturday for a fun day and then get a baby sitter for Saturday evening and we can go listen to some jazz at your favorite spot on main street in Media or we can go for dinner, drinks and dancing at Warmdaddy's"

"And you thought of that without any help from me?"

"I sure did." I just want us to get back to having fun and enjoying our family. I was thinking that I need to show you and the children that you are my first priority."

Mikki just stared at James and raised her eyebrows.

"Well let's all get ready for dinner and we can discuss our weekend plans later my dear"

"So was that face simply stating that I did a bad thing?

"No, James, I don't want you to think that way. I am glad that you are making decisions and showing us that we are your main priority, but I just wanted to have something to talk about after we put the children to bed, Mikki answered and then gave him a pat on the butt.

"Now go wash up and let's get ready for dinner, okay?"

"Sure babe, I'll be right back."

After dinner, Mikki and James gathered all of the children and escorted them upstairs to get their baths and get ready to go to bed. James had never removed his cell phone from his waist, so he was shocked that it went off.

"Hello?"

"James, I called and left 4 messages for you today and you haven't answered. I dare not call your house because I know that your wife or the babysitter does not relay the message. So why didn't you call me back?"

James took a deep breath before answering.

"Hello to you too mother, my day was fine, I am a little tired and I haven't had the chance to answer any voicemails because today was very hectic."

"I'm sorry son, but I just found out that you sister is being evicted and will have to move back here with me and Russell. I need some help getting her stuff out of the apartment before they put it out on the sidewalk and moving her and the girls back into the room here at the house that we made into Jordan's room."

"Well, what is Rita doing to correct her situation? Is she trying to pay the rent so that she can stay in her place? How is she going to work out the whole situation with transportation if she moves back home with you and her job is in West Chester?"

"She actually has no choice, Russell can't come up with the money for her to stay, and I don't have the money either." Unless you are willing to spot her the 3 months rent that she is behind or let her come and live with you and your family, she has no choice!"

"Mom, don't yell at me about your daughter's responsibility. When you said that she was moving, I didn't believe that she was ready for that big of a move." Rita was never given the responsibility of raising her kids or being a responsible adult. You always bailed her out. Come to think of it, didn't you pay first, last and security deposit for her?"

"Son, I am not going to talk about it, if we don't get her stuff, when she finally does move out of that back room, we are going to need to purchase new stuff again. I am not made of money, I can't take care of my house and Rita's at the same time and the best solution is for her to come here and maybe Russell will purchase her a car"

James could feel his blood pressure boiling but took a deep breath before responding.

"Okay, please tell me what sense that makes. Rita is a grown woman with two children and she can't pay her rent but your suggestion is that she keeps her job and her father will buy her a car? How about you take the money that you would use to purchase a car, give it to her as a loan so that she could not get evicted and stay in her apartment?"

"How about you tell your wife to sell your condo in Ocean City and then you can loan Rita the money to buy a house?"

"You really are kidding me right? I mean, this is really not my problem, I pay my bills on time and no one has to bail me out!"

"Son, we are family and when family is in trouble we should work to help each other out".

"Mom, you are really giving me a headache right now. I have a family here and they need to be taken care of and protected. I refuse to bail Rita out this time. If you and your husband decide that is what you want to do for your grown daughter, then so be it. Leave me out of this crazy equation".

"James, what is the problem, you have two incomes, two nice incomes for that matter and helping your sister out is not going to break the bank".

"Mother, let's get this straight, and I hope this is the last time that I have to tell you this, you have to stay out of my back pocket, my bank account, and any other money you think I have laying around. I have children that I need to raise and my income is for maintaining our family lifestyle- meaning James, Mikki, Jason, Steven, Shannon, Scott and Skyler".

"Yes, we are family but my first priority goes to the people that live here with me". "I really cannot be bothered with running to your defense every time you think you can run guilt trips on me about helping family out". "I almost lost my family because of your interference and I am currently working on correcting that situation now". "You and your husband have to figure this out for your daughter, and if that means her moving back in with you and you not giving her the money to stay in her apartment and later buying her a car, you made the decision and you have to deal with it".

James hung up the phone and raced up the stairs knowing that he had missed bath time but he could help Mikki put the boys to bed.

"Daddy, who was that on the phone," asked Steven

Mikki looked up but just shrugged her shoulders.

"It was your grand mom."

"Which one", Jason asked. "We have mommy's mom, we have Uncle Chris' mom, we have your mom and we have me-ma who is the great one!"

Mikki and James laughed.

"Okay you guys, enough questioning your daddy. It's time for bed because you have school tomorrow.

"Daddy, are we going to talk about going to Oasis on Saturday?"

"Yes guys, I promise".

James lipped Thank you to Mikki and they both gave kisses and hugs around to all of the boys before shutting out the lights.

James was a little upset that he did not get to kiss his two princesses but he decided that when he took Mikki out this weekend it was going to be the best night on the town.

The next morning, all was well at the Steven's house. The kids made it to school without issue. Mikki and James had a carefree morning without any bickering which had James was humming a tune. Just then, his cell phone went off. James walked over to his bed side table and picked it up to answer.

"Hello?"

"Hey, James this is Rita and I need your help".

"If this is about moving, or me lending you any money, no can do".

"James, this has nothing to do with money and I think that we really need to talk".

"Okay, Rita, what is this all about? I mean, we have never been really close and we have not always seen eye to eye on any topics, so why now?"

"James listen, you and I both know that mom is really manipulative when it comes to getting what she wants". "Especially if she thinks that she can get it from you. I am not losing my apartment, and mom wants me to move in with her because she needs the money that I would pay for rent".

"Ok, so what about Russell buying you a car if you moved back in with them?"

Rita laughed, "She told you that one too?"

"Look brother dear, I am not losing my apartment, my boyfriend and I are looking into buying a small house in Aldan, Glenolden, or West Chester. I am going to be starting school in the fall of next year and I want to make sure that Diamond and Sierra are settled in a good school district".

"I really don't know what to say, Rita?"

"Don't be so shocked, brother; I know that in the past, I have acted like a clown". "I have had time to be on my own and be a good parent to my girls and see that I want so much for them as well as myself". "I have not been under mom's influence and she doesn't like it one bit". "She needs to have control and I can't allow her to ruin my life or run it for that matter".

"Rita, I always wanted what was best for you but you seemed to always take the other road".

"Yes, but my counselor, told me that a lot of my impulsivity came from wanting attention from mom that I wasn't getting". "I am too old to try to get attention from mom". "In her own sick twisted way, I know that she loves all of us and wants what's best for us". "But in some way she thinks that anything we achieve should include her but not surpass the things that she has done in life".

"Okay, you're going to counseling? When did this begin?"

"I have been in counseling, for almost a year now. I decided that I needed to see someone because I felt out of control". "Being in counseling has helped me think of the consequences for my actions as well as being responsible for Diamond and Sierra". "It helped me realize that I needed to move on and act like an adult and begin doing adult things and taking care of myself".

"I'm proud of you Rita. So what did you really call for today?"

"Well, brother dear, what I need help with, is that Russell, Jr. is planning on transferring from Community College to Delaware State and Jordan has been accepted there as well. Both of them graduate in June. You know both of them decided to work right after high school and not go to college but both of them will have their associate's degree in June and want to go away and finish their degrees. My dad is ecstatic that both of his sons are going away to school and really needs your help with filling out the financial aid information for the both of them".

"My dad would like to meet with you, so that you can give him insight on what they will need because what I have found out is that, my dad has been saving for all of us to go to school". "But you know, I had Diamond at 16 and then Sierra 18 months later, college for me was put on the back burner".

"Okay, I need to sit down, Russell, your dad is being involved with all of you?"

"J, my dad has always tried to be the best dad he could be to all of us, even to you. But Jackson was always a good father to you although he only saw you on the weekends. But there was also the fact that mommy made you do everything, that my dad should have done and he felt resentful. He was glad that once you went to college he could do what he was supposed to as our father and not have mommy always calling on you".

"Do you actually think that I wanted to be the man of the house at a young age Rita?"

"I know you didn't but it was hard for you to sit back and let others do because of your take charge attitude". "I am just grateful, that you didn't become jaded about relationships and married Mikki". "I think that she is good for you and you better do whatever you need to do to make your marriage work."

"I'm trying sis, I really am". "Well, tell your dad that I would be willing to speak to him anytime, or he can just come to the house and whatever paper work he has, I will help him with".

"I'm glad that you'll help out. I will keep you posted on my house hunt with Terrence and we should get together real soon and act like we are adult siblings". "I missed out on a lot and you do have a good adult relationship with Chris and Janice, so I think we need to work on ours as well".

"Rita, I would really like that and I am really proud of you. I love you sis".

"I know J, and I love you too. Be happy and make sure you work on your marriage because, I know that you and Mikki are in counseling".

"Oh, you do?"

"Yes, I saw Mikki coming out of Ratcliff's office when I was on my way for my counseling session".

"You see Brenda too?"

"No, Brenda did my intake along with her social worker, but I see her partner Mike Jamison". I heard about the work they that do together and I know about Brenda's TMBP thing she is working on". "But after my intake and evaluation, I was chosen for the work that Mike is doing with Brenda and Terrence and I go to Mike for counseling as well".

"Couples counseling? I thought that you two were just boyfriend and girlfriend?"

"J, I am 4 months pregnant with Terrence's child, we plan on having a future together". "We have known each other for almost 2 years and he is good to the girls as well as me". "We are planning to get married sometime after the baby is born but I needed him to understand the mental damage that I am trying to correct so that we can sustain a healthy relationship, similar to what Mikki's parents or to what Terrence's parents have had for years"

"I can respect that Rita, but what does mom have to say about all that?"

"You know what, I didn't check with her on that". "I have learned that my life does not have to be directly tied to moms". "That's her doing. "In order for me to have control over my life, I can't always include mom in the decisions that I make". "I'm almost thirty and I did not do much of anything without including mom in the decisions I made and sometimes, I just allowed her to make the decision, so that she could have control". "And since I moved into my apartment and have been working on me, I just don't need the stress". "My life is cool without all of the drama that mom wants to lay on me". "You never know, I may be just as bourgeois as your wife one day!"

"You know what, you are funny Rita". "I'm can't tell you how proud I am of you". "And Mikki isn't bourgeois as you put it, she just always wants to do what's right". "And I can guarantee that some of the things you and mom used to laugh about that she did with the kids, you are doing now".

"No, Mikki is really cool and I hope one day that we can be friends and at least have a cordial relationship". "I respect her and I found that I look up to her because she did a lot of things that I couldn't because I had children at an early age". "But when you get caught up in false promises and being controlled that's what happens; and I am doing my best to make my life better for me and all that surround me". "Well, I really do have to go, Terrence and I are looking at a house in West

Chester in about an hour and I want to run to the store before I do that". "Hope to talk to you soon and thanks again big brother".

"No, thank you Rita".

James put the phone down and walked into the office to get his laptop and make his way to work. His sister had given him a lot of insight on his mom as well as a lot to think about before his next session with Brenda.

Mikki

Mikki had a long day at work today. She was on her way to her session with Brenda but felt very apprehensive about it. She knew that in order for this to work, that she had to put her best foot forward and not think negatively about the outcome. Mikki walked into Brenda's office and spoke with the receptionist and took a seat to wait for Brenda to come out and get her.

"Hey Mikki, why don't you come on back to my office?"

"Hi, Brenda, how are u?"

"I'm fine, I really like those shoes Mikki, let's see, did the Diva princess get them from Gucci?"

"I'm going to disregard that you called me the Diva princess, Brenda, because I know for a fact someone who drops a mint in Lord & Taylor when she should only be going in for one thing!"

They both laughed and sat down in Brenda's office.

Mikki was glad that although, Brenda was her counselor, mediator or whatever, they had a good relationship and were on the track to becoming friends.

"So, Mikki, how has it been since the last time we had a session?"

"Well, Bren, I have to tell, you, we have had no bad arguments, I haven't really heard that my mother in-law has called making outrageous requests but sometimes I feel like I am just waiting for the other foot to drop".

"You mean like on edge?" "Or that you are just lying in wait for something big happen?"

"Yeah, I think that because James and I have always compromised and or changed plans that have subsequently lead to a big blow up about his mom, and it hasn't happened in a while, I just prepared for the next one to be very big".

"Well what if there was a change and you didn't have to compromise your time or your plans and things went smoothly for a long time to come. How would you feel?"

"I don't know, I guess that I am so programmed to rearranging our schedules for his mom I wouldn't know how to react. I'm still expecting it to be the way it always was".

"Okay, tell me about your family dynamic growing up. I know about you being the oldest of the 5 children that your parents had together and your older sister Leslie being from a relationship that your father had. But what was it like being in your family?"

"Well, first off, Leslie is not that much older than I, there is 18 months between the two of us, and mom is essentially the mother that she has always known". "Leslie's mother from what we all know from my parents, died when she was about 3 weeks old". "My grandmother says that she died from hemorrhaging from giving birth".

"My mom and dad were college sweethearts and Leslie's mom was someone that my dad dated on and off before he met my mom". "When my parents announced that they were a couple, Leslie's mom announced that she was happy for them, but that she was pregnant and that she was going to keep the baby". "My dad said that he would support her but that he was in love with my mom". "My mom and Leslie's mom were friendly and my mom was actually named god-mother when Leslie was born".

"But what about growing up in your house with all of those kids?"

"Well you have to remember, my parents did not have any more children until I was about 5". "After my sister Monica, Jamie came two years later and then my brother's the knock out twins came three years later after that".

"We were always close and my parents were very heavily involved in everything that we did". "My dad always made us volunteer somewhere, all of the girls danced at Philadanco beginning when they were 5, we did girl scouts, the boys did cub scouts and we took turns at playing an instrument".

"Do you think that all families were like yours?"

"I think when I was younger, I was jaded and thought that, but my friend Michele helped me change my thinking".

"How so?"

"Michele was the only child of her parents until she was about 14". "Michele, although she was younger than I, was very smart so she was in a lot of my classes because she had got skipped". "Michele always did everything that we did, family vacations, danced at Philadanco community events and we always saw her parents cheering her on". "It wasn't until she found out that her mom was having another baby, did we find out how not happy her household was".

"Go, on".

"Michele's mom came over to tell us that she was expecting and how excited she was and that she was due in December during a family cookout". "After, Michele's mom made the announcement, Michele asked if we could go upstairs and hang out in me and Leslie's room with Leslie and Gina to talk". "When we got upstairs to talk, she just started crying about how she didn't want her mom to have the baby". "We thought that she was just being a brat because she was the only child and we told her that it would be good for her parents because at the time we were about to start 11th grade".

"That's when she broke the news to us, that her dad although he supports her in everything that she does, had cheated on her mom in the past and because of that she did not think that he was a great husband to her mother". "She was hoping that when she graduated from high school that, her mom would leave her dad". "We all asked her why she felt that way and she thought it was for the best".

"Okay, so now back to you?" " I told you during your intake meeting that your first relationships affect relationships, later in life, so how do you think that your relationship with your father mentored the expectations that you have for James?"

"I don't think that my relationship with my father had a lot to do with the expectations that I placed on James". "I mean, they always say that you tend to date men that have characteristics of your father- but I had a lot of father figures in my life that influenced me besides my dad". "Not only that, my dad always made it known that when we began dating that we should always respect ourselves and not let any man disrespect us". "My dads always let us know that we had control over our dating lives not the men we were dating". "Don't get me wrong, my sister's and I are daddy's girls to the core and we grew up knowing that he would protect us and our mother at all costs". "But I still believe that I had a myriad of father figures to look at".

"Like who?"

"Well, let's begin with Michele's dad, he was like a second father to all of us that were really good friends with Michele". "He would talk to us and give us advice, he would fuss at us if we were getting into trouble and we were around him a lot". "I also had all of my father's brother's because he is the youngest of 5 boys, my granddad as well as my god-father".

"Do you think that you expected James to be just like any of the men in your life?"

"I'll tell you this much, I expected James to protect and care for me like I had seen in all of the married couples that I knew of". "But I also felt that he would be good to me because he was good to his mother".

"So, you had no expectations at all?"

"Again, part of me fell in love with James because of the way he treated and cared for his mother and part of me wanted that for me". "I mean, for most of my college years, I dated Kevin and I later found out that he treated me with respect when we were in the same city but because I went to school in Pittsburgh and he was in Philadelphia when I was out of sight, I was out of mind". "So I can say that I wanted him to protect me and honor me like he did his mother". "But James and my relationship blossomed, first as friendship; we didn't even sleep together until we had been together for almost a year".

"Really? Why so long?

" I think part of it was because when we first began dating, I was so like we are friends, that we would hug and give each other chaste little kisses and the fact that I had just started working, we really didn't spend a lot of time together for the first 5 months of us being an official couple". "Then we always had to re-arrange a lot of things so that he could run errands for his mom or drive her somewhere, that it was never the right time or moment". "James always made me feel protected and important to him when we were together so we had a lot of time to just get to know each other and find out what really made each other tick before adding sex into the equation". "But that all changed when he asked me to marry him".

"How long had you guys been dating when he asked you to marry him?"

"10 months to be exact". "We were leaving my parents house after a family dinner to celebrate something special and we were heading to meet Michele, Gina, Mike and some of our other friends at Lagoon to play pool and have some drinks but we needed to stop at my apartment so that I could change into some jeans".

"While he was waiting for me to change my jeans he wrote me this note like the ones from grade school that said will you marry me, check yes or no and folded me a paper ring with some notebook paper". "He had another ring in his back pocket but he had gotten some Pear cider from Harry & David, Haribou Gummi bears and plastic wine glasses from the store. He set up this on my coffee table along with a plaid table cloth and was sitting on the floor waiting for me".

"Sounds cute and cheap?"

"Well, frugal is more like it, but it was the thought that he was creative and I never saw it coming". "So when I walked back into my living room, he asked me to come and sit on his lap so that we could talk". "He passes me the note, but when I started crying, he told me that although we promised to take our relationship slow, that he could never see his life without me because I made him feel special and that no one had ever made him feel important, like I did". "He also told me that he love d that our relationship could be simple or exciting and that he was glad that I felt comfortable with him in all aspects in my life and that was why he asked me to marry him".

"So, you marked off yes and as they say the rest was history right?"

"No, not necessarily, my parents, knew what he had planned to do, because earlier that night at dinner, he had spoke to both my father and mother privately and told them that although we had only been dating for 10 months he would be willing to wait and have a long engagement". "But his mother was a whole different story".

"What happened when he told her?"

"Well, James had decided that we would tell her together because we were going to go to brunch with her in a couple of days, but when we did tell her, I never thought that she would have the response that she did!"

"What did she say?"

"Well we took her to Hibachi, because James said that she had never been even when his fraternity hosted a jazz brunch she had never attended". "So after placing our orders, James tells his mom that we have an announcement". "But before we could tell her that we were engaged, she jumps up and hugs me telling me that she was happy for us and when the due date was!"

"Were you shocked?"

"Shocked can't even describe what I felt. James had to calm his mother down and tell her that I was not pregnant but that we were engaged and that we were going to have a long engagement". "If you could have only seen the look on his mom's face". "After a few minutes of just staring at us, she asked to look at the ring but the reaction to the ring was one I will never ever forget".

"What did she say?"

"She kindly looked at James and asked him how much did he spend on the ring and that he never brought her anything like that!"

"She then proceeded to ask him if he went to see a lawyer for a pre-nuptial agreement, because she didn't want me to take him for all of his money". "She then went on to explain that if I was having a baby she would not even mention a pre-nuptial but she never thought that James would even consider marriage". "So if he decided that he wanted to marry me, she just wanted to make sure that he was protected".

"Okay, she didn't say it was nice?"

"No and I think her reaction not only made James mad but he was a little bit embarrassed". "She finally recovered and noticed that

James was a little upset, and then said that she was happy for us but that she only mentioned anything about a prenuptial agreement because she knew that there were some of the doctor's that she worked with who when they married nurses that they worked with they made them sign prenuptials and that was the last time that we, meaning her, James and I did anything together".

"So did you and James ever have a conversation about his mother's reaction?"

"Well, the rest of the night progressed without incident, his mom kept talking about how she was going to tell Russell that James had taken her somewhere nice to eat and she was so upset that he never took her anywhere nice". "James was particularly quiet for the rest of the evening until after we dropped her off".

"Well what did he have to say?"

"Well at first he said nothing, and we had planned to go back to my apartment and watch some The Thin Man Movies and just relax for the rest of the day". "James was in the bedroom changing his clothes and I was in the living room and I hear him on the phone". "I walked into the bedroom and James is talking to his father, Jackson about how upset he was that his mother embarrassed him". "I walked out of the room to give him time to vent to his father and a little bit later his sister

Janice and his brother Chris showed up and we all hung out for the rest of the night".

"So you two never had a conversation at all?"

"Sorta kind of".

"What does that mean?"

"Well about three days later, we were at a function that was honoring his company's work in the community and I was there to support him and I met his boss". "When his boss came over to meet me, he makes a joke about me being the lovely woman that should get James to sign a prenuptial". "What I found out afterwards is his boss at that time was friends with my father's brother Milton and he already knew me".

"Well after we left the banquet". "James starts apologizing about how sorry he was that his mother embarrassed me when we were out and that he would make sure that it never happened again". "I told him not to worry about it and that I would try hard to work on our relationship so that we would be able to get along". "He told me not to worry about it". "And that was the last discussion that we ever had about any bad behavior from his mother".

"Okay, Mikki, your time is almost up, but I want to give you an assignment to do, before we meet again". "I want you to invite your mother in law to lunch and have a little girls talk".

"Brenda, I will do the assignment, but I have in my head this is leading to disaster".

"All, I want you to do is, take her out to lunch and it can be on her terms, and just have conversation". "Nothing controversial, like her dislike of you being married to her son". "But try to pick her brain and see what makes her tick".

"I will do the assignment, but if I end up on Channel 6 news make sure you take the blame for this one!" "I will follow through with the assignment, but you have been warned!"

"I am seeing James for his first group session later and I will know if you two are ready to meet for couples counseling". "But couples counseling is done along with my partner Mike Jamison who runs the other study that is part of the TMBP dissertation".

"Okay, Brenda, thanks and I will see you in two weeks".

The two of them hugged and walked out of Brenda's office to the waiting area.

Once Mikki was out in the waiting area, she thought she saw a familiar face sitting in the corner of the waiting area. She walked a short distance to the small sitting area, and who was sitting there but Russell, Rita and Rita's boyfriend Terrence. The three of them were in a hushed conversation and didn't see Mikki approach.

"Ahem, Hello Rita, Russell and Terrence, how are you?"

All three of them looked up with surprise that Mikki was standing before them.

"Please tell me why you are here in the same counseling office as James and I?"

"Mikki, Terrence and I have been going through couples counseling for the last 2 months with Mike Jamison". "I have also been going through individual counseling with Mike for almost a year now" Rita said.

"Oh, I guess James and I are not the only crazy ones around here, Huh?"

Russell got up and walked over to Mikki and gave her a hug. "Mikki, it's good to see you and no you and James are not crazy". "You are going through a rough patch and I think it is a good idea for you two to be in counseling". "I wish my wife was here as moral support for me or for that matter to go through counseling herself- but I'm here because I also have begun therapy with Mike Jamison".

"Okay, but Rita, I thought you were moving back home with your parents?"

"Girl, are you crazy?" "Who is spreading that rumor?" "Terrence, and I are looking for a house and I am 4 months pregnant". "As long as we can get our act together, we will be walking that aisle like you and my brother".

"Okay, I need to sit down, because I am starting to feel like I'm in the twilight zone".

"Mikki, you may have overheard that I was moving back, but I'm not". "I'll let my brother fill you in on what is really going on because I talked to him earlier today but the little miserable brat that splashed juice in your face at your wedding is long gone".

"Russell, Terrence and Rita, Mike is ready for you guys in his office" the receptionist stated.

"Well, it was good seeing you all, Rita give me a call if you want to talk".

"I sure will Mikki, I'll give you a call later in the week".

"It was good seeing you both, Terrence and Russell".

They both nodded their heads and followed the receptionist to the counselor's office.

Mikki picked up her briefcase and then walked out of the building to her car. She needed to get to the office so that she could sit down and digest what she saw and what she heard from Brenda today.

Once she got to the office, she left a message on James' voicemail at work to let him know that she arrived at work and was done her session. She knew that they were going to talk later because she had to explain what she saw while at counseling today.

She thought about the assignment that Brenda gave her and figured that she would give her mother in law a call to see if she could make arrangements for them to go to lunch on Saturday. She picked up the phone and dialed a number that she dialed infrequently.

After the third ring, her mother in law answered.

"Hello, Regina- how are you today?"

"Who is this?"

"Regina this is Mikki and I was calling to see if you wanted to go out to lunch on Saturday with me?"

"Who is this?"

Mikki took a deep breath. "Regina, this is Mikki, James' wife".

"I know that you're my son's wife, don't be stupid!" "I was just surprised that you of all people would be calling me with your bourgeois self!"

"Okay, well how about lunch on Saturday?"

"If, I agree, are you going to let me pick the spot?" "And you're treating right?"

"Yes, you tell me the place, I will pick up the tab and I was hoping that we could have lunch and chat".

"Okay, well, I tell you what, I have never gotten around to making Russell take me to *Ms. Tootsies* that new soul food place on South Street". "So you make the reservations and I will be ready to go by 2pm on Saturday. Deal?"

"Deal, I will pick you up at 1 on Saturday that will give us time to get from your house to Ms. Tootsies and find parking on South Street".

"I will be ready and I will see you then".

Mikki hung up but in her mind she knew that this was not going to be an easy lunch.

Mikki then called and made reservations for 3pm at Ms. Tootsies for Saturday, because she knew her mother in law was not going to make this easy for her.

James

James was tired from his group session with Brenda as well as from all of the information that he learned today. He just wanted to go home and relax. But before he could go home and relax with his family, he needed to go and talk to his mom. "Before, I do anything, let me call Mikki and tell her that I will be running a little late".

"Hello, this is Mikki Stevens".

"Hi, Mrs. Stevens, this is Mr. Stevens".

"How was your day?"

"All is well, I just wanted to let you know that I was going to be late tonight". "I am going to stop off at my mother's because she wanted to talk to me and then I will be home".

"Should I wait up?"

"If you wait up, can you please wait up in something red and run me some bath water?"

"That I can do, but please give me a call to let me know when you are close to home so that I can run the water so that it is warm and not lukewarm".

"I can do that."

"Mikki, just know that I love you and I can't wait until we get a chance to talk tonight".

"I love you, too". "And I have some things that I want to discuss with you as well". "Drive safe".

"She agreed to be wearing red, okay Mom- I'm on my way but you need to make this conversation quick!"

James picked up his briefcase and walked out his office to make the drive to his mother's house.

Once he arrived at his mother's house, he parked his car and used his key to go in. He dropped his brief case on the sofa and yelled for his mom.

"Hold your horses, I'm coming and why are you yelling in my house boy?" "Listen, come back in the kitchen, I am preparing dinner and talking to an old friend of yours".

James walked in the kitchen and was surprised to see his old high school girlfriend Terri, sitting at his mom's kitchen table peeling potatoes. "Hey, Terri, long time no see?"

Terri got up and wiped her hands on the dish towel that she had on her lap. "Hey, James, she said with a big smile and gave him a hug". "I just stopped by to see your mom while I was in town visiting and brought over pictures of my children and the new house that I just purchased in Bear, Delaware".

"Isn't that nice James that Terri still comes by to see me? I always thought that you two would have some nice children together".

"Miss Regina, now you know that James and I are way in the past". "I just always considered you my extended family and that is why, I always come by and see you". "I will stop by even more, because I am closer to Philly now that I don't live in Texas anymore".

"Well, what made you move back to the east coast?"

"James, my son will be 18 in March and he has been accepted to the University of Delaware with a full scholarship and my husband is will be stationed at Dover Air Force Base for the next two years and what I hope will be his last years in the Air Force, so it was easier for us to make the transition and be closer to family and friends".

"And how old are your other children, well we have been blessed, my twins are 6 and my husband John has a sixteen year old daughter and a 13 year old son, so we are one big happy blended family".

James took a long look at Terri and could not help but remember that at one time he thought that they would be married with children. She hadn't changed much from what he remembered except that at 37 and 36 respectively they could both say that they had 5 children. But Terri reminded him of kept woman, she was average height, with brown eyes, dark brown hair that appeared to be salon done with highlights, she had on from what he could tell, a button down Burberry Brand shirt in beige, with black flat front slacks and black riding boots to complete the outfit. James knew that Terri had never really wanted to work a day in her life, and she told him so when, he went off to college. That was one of the reasons why they broke it off, because in his eyes, she had no ambition at all.

"James, I was looking at pictures of Terri's family and her oldest son is very handsome, if I do say so myself". "He reminds me a lot like you when you were that age?"

James lifted his brow and walked over to the table where he saw the pictures that Terri had left out of her family. He didn't know what his mom was trying to insinuate, but he knew for sure that Terri's son was not his son at all because he and Terri were not together at the time that she got pregnant.

"Mom, I see that you have company, so how about I come over on Saturday and we can have our little heart to heart?"

"No, son I can't do it on Saturday, I have an appointment in the afternoon, and I know that you probably have activities planned with the children for the weekend". "How about I call you and set up another time to talk to you?" "Or you can stay for dinner and catch up with Terri, I am making your favorite, homemade fried chicken, mashed potatoes and greens".

"Well, I guess, I can stay for dinner, I did tell Mikki that I would be a little late and I haven't eaten dinner yet". "Why not?"

"Okay, it's settled- Terri put those potatoes in the pan so that I can mash them and I just put the biscuits in the oven!" "You two go sit at the dining room table where I put some fresh lemonade out and I'll be right there!"

Terri and James just shrugged and did what she asked and went into the dining room.

"So, how is married life treating you James?" " I can say for me, I was surprised that your mom got her hooks out of your long enough for you to get married?"

"What do you mean about that Terri?"

"James, all of us growing up knew that you were a dedicated son to your mother, but me in particular never thought you would get married to anyone, because at the drop of a hat, you would rearrange your schedule to make sure that your mom was okay and that things that you did for her got done over anything else". "I was glad that you did at least live on campus when you started college".

"Why is that Terri?"

"Because, to me, I thought you would get a little more freedom to do things that you wanted to do without having the time constraints of managing a family".

"Well, I can say for one Terri, that I love my wife, with all of my heart and she is my world". "I almost lost her and I don't plan on losing her or my children because I am not putting my family first". "I am learning some hard lessons about myself". "I know that I am good at managing a family but I surely can't be the king of two castles". "I owe it to my wife and my children to make sure that they know that".

"Well, I can see that your mom is going to task with you about that?"

"What do you mean Terri?"

"Well, when I said that I never thought you of all people would get married?" "Well let me tell you why I really broke it off with you during your freshman year of college".

"Okay, I'm listening".

"Your freshman year of college was during my senior year of high school and we were supposed to go my senior fall dance". "In the summer when you were away, I had met my son's father and we would talk on the phone, hang out and I really started to like him". "I didn't tell you about him because initially we were just friends". "Our relation grew and around the time that the fall dance was approaching, I wanted to take him instead of you but I was still up in the air about it because I still knew that I had feelings for you but I wasn't sure where we stood because we hadn't spent a lot of time together because you were busy in school".

"I don't see where this leading Terri".

"Just bear with me, because I want to explain it to you". "I came to talk to your mom about what I was feeling because you and I had been dating for 2 years and we had talked about marriage later after we both finished college and all of our dreams and I explained that to your mom that as well". "She told me that it was a possibility that we would have children, but she never thought that you would get married". "She then went on to tell me about your father and how he broke her heart and got married to Chris' mom and that typically the apple don't fall to far from the tree, you would probably wind up doing the same to me that your father did to her".

"She never explained that she and my father were never dating and that they were just sneaking around when she just happened to get pregnant with me?"

"After listening to her entire story, James, my heart was hurting". " I just left and when I got home, that is when I made the decision to break up with you". "My son's father preyed on the fact that I was hurting and told me that he would never do anything like that to me and I got pregnant with my son the night of the fall dance because after the dance, we went to a hotel and spent the night".

"So although, you never talked to me about what my mom said to you, you had it set up in your mind that I was going to hurt you like Jackson supposedly hurt my mom?"

"Why would I think she would lie to me?"

"But you knew my character, did you think that I would just talk about marriage, my dreams and children because I wanted you to just have my children?"

"James, I knew better after the fact because once, I was pregnant my son's father did not want to be bothered with me, I had a lot of time to think about the people who really had supported me". "Your mom was very helpful to me when I was pregnant, and very encouraging, partly because she thought that my son was yours". "But my mom also brought it to my attention that you always treated me with respect".

"Well, I am glad to have had this talk with you Terri". "Does my mom still think that your son is mines?"

"I don't believe so, because his father is related to Diamond and Sierra's father".

"You mean, your son is Diamond and Sierra's brother?"

"No, James, my son is Diamond and Sierra's cousin". "My son's father is Sierra and Diamond's uncle".

"Well, Terri I thank you for all that we talked about, let's just have a good dinner with my mom and I will have a talk with her later". "You really did give me a lot of insight on my mom".

"No problem and I hope to meet your wife sometime soon".

"I think that we can work that out because I really think she would like you". "You two have the same taste in clothes".

Just then James' mom walked in with a platter of chicken, so the three of them could sit down and eat. The rest of the night flowed with funny stories of the past and good food but James knew that he had to deal with his mother, but he just didn't know what to do.

Mikki

Mikki had dosed off right after putting the children to bed in their sitting room. She lifted her head up to see that it was almost 9:30 and she still had not heard from James. She decided that maybe his conversation with his mother had run into overtime, so she decided that she would take a shower and get ready for bed. She went down the hall to check the children were still asleep and then went back into her bathroom and started her shower.

After her shower she brushed her teeth and picked up her journal that Brenda have given her to write in and placed it in her bedside table.

After using her favorite Body Cream from Annick Goutal, she put on comfortable PJ's wrapped her hair in a silk bonnet and went to bed.

By the time James did come in the house, Mikki was close to being in deep sleep but she did hear him start the shower and then climb in bed. Mikki could only hope that after her lunch with his mother, they all would be a little better off.

In the morning, the alarm went off extra early for a Saturday in their house, Mikki knew that they Steven and Scott had a basketball games at 10:15 at the community center, Shannon and Skylar had dance class from 9:30 – 11:45 and Jason had Gymboree from 9:45 – 10:30. The plan was that James would take the girls and Jason and drop them off and she would take Scott and Steven to their game and James would then meet her to watch. After the boy's games, James would go pick up Jason and the girls and meet her back at the house for to make sure all of the children had showers and be ready for nap time.

James had planned to take the children along with Mike and MJ, to Oasis for bowling and rock climbing in the afternoon while Mikki went on the lunch date with his mom. Gina was to meet them at the house later and they were going to all have an adult night of spades once Mikki returned.

Mikki rolled over and hit the alarm for the last time it was 7:30 and she knew that she had to get up and get breakfast ready as wells as get everyone in her house moving.

"Good morning, James time to get up!"

"Do you have to be so cheerful, this morning?

"I'm not being cheerful, I am just using my authoritative voice, so that those who come in late at night will still get an early start".

James just put the covers back over his head and groaned. Just then, they heard footsteps.

"Oh, no- just what I need, the triple threat children up early and raring to go".

"Well, you better get up, because, Jason is excited about Gymboree, because some of his friends from daycare go".

James turned around and grabbed Mikki around her waist and pulled her close. "So, I guess there is no chance for some morning loving? And what happened to you being ready and waiting for me in something red?"

"James, you came home way to late, and you know on Fridays, I am asleep as early as the kids are".

Just then, their bedroom door swung open and there stood what James had called the triple threat, Shannon, Skylar and Jason.

"What's up sprouts? Good morning!"

"Good morning, Mommy and Daddy, the three of the answers in unison.

"Okay, guys, since you are already up, let's get you in the shower for your day ahead". "Daddy and Uncle Mike are going to take you later this afternoon, to Oasis and then we will have some more family time this evening because MJ, Auntie Gina and Uncle Mike are going to stay with us until Sunday afternoon".

"Does that mean Auntie Gina is going to make flap jacks?" asked Skylar.

"They are called pannycakes, not flap jacks", shouted Jason.

"Guys, settle down, Jason auntie Gina calls them flap jacks, but you can also call them pancakes but yes, she is going to make her special apple cinnamon pancakes while she is here". "Now let's go get your brothers up so that we can have breakfast and get ready for a good day".

"Okay mom".

The day went relatively without a hitch. The boys won their basketball game, Skylar and Shannon talked excitedly about dance class and Jason was ecstatic about being in Gymboree with his friend Nasir. Once they got back to the house, Mikki and James made lunch for the children and shortly after the twins and Jason were asleep and Steven and

Scott were in the family room watching TV, Mikki went upstairs to get ready for lunch with her mother in law.

James walked into their bedroom to find Mikki had finished dressing in a red blouse and black slacks. "Hey, where are you headed? You are not going out to meet some other man are you?"

Mikki threw a pillow at him. "No, silly, I am taking your mother to Ms. Tootsie's for a late lunch".

"You and my mom?" " What gives?" "My mom said that she had an appointment, but I definitely did not know that you two were having a girl's day out".

"Well, I definitely would not call it a girl's day out, but Brenda suggested that I extend the olive leaf to your mom and go to lunch to see if we could at least try and be cordial".

"And Gina is not going with you to be the buffer?"

"No, I am not taking Gina with us, Brenda already told me that it just had to be me and your mom, so we are going to have a good lunch and that's it". "Also, Gina said that because MJ had basketball this morning, they would not be getting to the house until about 2".

"What time are your reservations?"

"I made them for three because I know in the past that your mom has not been ready on time and I told her that I would be there to pick her up no later than 1:15".

"But my mom is not that far from Ms. Tootsies, Mik why 3 o'clock?"

"Well, I still need to get parking near Ms. Tootsies and sometimes people just show up and then you have to wait". "I don't want to inconvenience your mom and have her standing outside because they don't have a table ready for us".

"Good thinking". "Now before you leave, let me spin you around and take a good luck at you." "You are looking so good Mrs. Stevens and you have on my favorite color".

"Well, I'm glad that you like but it is now 12:45 and it takes me at least 20 minutes to your mom's house and I don't want to be late".

James grabbed Mikki and gave her a kiss on the lips and then winked. "I will see you when you got home, so we can beat Gina and Mike in spades".

"Okay, and make sure that when you and Mike make your beer run, you get me some Merlot or Shirazz".

"I will honey and be nice to my mom!"

"I am always nice".

Mikki got into her truck and made the drive from their house to her mother in laws house with ease. Once she found a parking spot, she knocked on the door. Russell Jr. answered the door.

"Hey Mikki, good to see you". "What brings you to my mom's house this afternoon?"

"Your mom and I are going to lunch at Ms. Tootsies". "We have reservations".

"You and my mom?" " I am shocked by that one". "As long as you and J have been together, I would have never thought my mom would be caught dead alone with you".

Mikki walked into the living room and had a seat on the couch. "You think I hate your mother that much RJ?"

"No, I never thought that you hated my mother, but it was more the other way around". "Because my mom treated you the way she did is one of the reasons I don't bring any woman that I'm dating around her!"

"So are you going to continue to not bring women around your mom because of the way she treats me?"

"Naw, Mikki I am serious about my current girlfriend Aliya, but I need to finish school and get a good job". "I decided to go to college a little late and I want to finish up at Delaware State once I graduate with my Associates from Community College in May". "Once I finish that and get a good job, I want to make sure that I wife Aliya". "But because, I have grown up watching my parent's dysfunctional marriage and I see from Aliya's parents and from you and my brother that marriage can work I see that it can be in the cards for me and Aliya".

"I'm glad for you RJ, can you please tell your mom that I am here so that we can make our reservations?"

"Sure, and Mikki good luck today, you sure going to need it!"

Russell walked up the stairs to tell his mom that Mikki was downstairs and after grabbed his jacket off the back of the chair in the dining room and took his keys off the key hook and left.

A few minutes later, Regina came down the stairs with her jacket and Mikki checked out what she was wearing. Usually when she saw Regina, Mikki often saw her in scrubs because she worked at the hospital. Regina had her hair styled with short layered curls in the front and the back of her hair flowed down past her shoulders. She was wearing a denim pencil skirt with a matching denim jacket and a floral print shirt. She wore black loafers and was carrying her navy blue coach bag that Mikki knew that James had given her as a gift for Christmas a few years back and had a bigger coach duffel bag on her arm as well.

"Well, Mikki, I am ready to go, but if you don't mind". "After we eat, I need to go to work because one of my co-workers had to work a double and was supposed to get off at 3 but the person that was supposed to come in at 3 called out". "I told her once we were finished our lunch that I would relieve her but it would be closer to five". "She was okay with staying the additional 2 hours but did not feel up to staying until 11 because she has been there since 11 last night".

"Okay, the hospital is not too far from Ms. Tootsies so I don't have a problem with dropping you off".

They both left the house and walked the short distance to the car and got in. The drive to Ms. Tootsies was done without a lot of idle chatter between the two women, but Mikki had a feeling that Regina would be full of chatter once they got to the restaurant.

Once they got to the restaurant, Regina acted like a kid in the candy store. "Mikki, this place is very nice". "It is also kind of small but I'm glad that you made reservations".

"We may have to wait for a few minutes, I made the reservations for 3 o'clock instead of 2 because they are often crowded and I wanted to make sure that we had a table".

"That's fine, but I hope they seat us soon, because I just looked at that girl's plate and that okra, corn and tomatoes look very good".

After waiting about 15 minutes the ladies were seated and Mikki noticed that there were 3 seats instead of two. When Mikki went to motion to the waitress, Regina explained why there were three seats instead of two.

"Mikki, when I knew that we were coming to Ms. Tootsies, I knew that the reservation was going to be under your last name, I changed the reservation to three, because I invited someone here for you to meet".

Mikki raised her eyebrow, "And who might that be?"

"Mikki, I invited Terri, James' old girlfriend from high school". "She just recently moved back into the area and she has always been like my second daughter". "I also thought that it was time to let you know that her 17 year old son, Micah may be my grandson".

"So you believe that Terri's son is James' son?"

"I don't believe, I know and I told James that last night".

"James never talked to me about finding out that he was Micah's father".

"And why should he, anything that he does for Micah will be none of your concern".

"Why wouldn't Micah be any of my concern, if he is James' child?" "My children would be his siblings and Micah would have to interact with them as well".

"I don't believe that Terri is interested in Micah being a part of your family Mikki". "I just think that she wants Micah to have a relationship with her and James".

"Are you kidding me?" " Do you really think that after Micah not being a part of James life for all this time that James is going to allow for Micah not to interact with his children?"

"James and I decided last night that he just needs to make sure that he spends time with Micah alone to get to know his son". "I told James that it was best that Micah doesn't blend in with you and the children because that would be detrimental to Micah". "Micah already has a mother in Terri and he does not need to have a step mother as well".

"Are you kidding me, did you think that my children need to know their brother, if this is James' child?" "Or because you dislike me so much, you did not consider that your grandchildren are just important as Micah?"

"James and I talked about that as well, we decided that the children would meet Micah later, but only on the condition that you were included in those visitations".

Just then someone tapped Mikki on her shoulder and she turned around to see that it was her old colleague, Morgan Fredericks. "Hello, Morgan, how are you? How is life in Atlanta treating you?"

Morgan stood about 6'3 with a dark coffee complexion with broad shoulders. He wore his curly hair cropped short and was dressed nicely in a cream cashmere sweater, navy blue mock neck and dark navy blue jeans and black Timberland boots. He had his black wool blazer slung over his arm.

Morgan pulled Mikki into a hug and answered, "Atlanta is good, I am just up here for the weekend to spend some time with my grandmother and my aunts". "You know that the job market for teachers and principals is booming and with your credentials you would find a job in no time".

"Morgan, I would like you to meet my mother in law Regina we were here for a late lunch this afternoon".

"Nice to meet you ma'am". "Well, I see that your food is arriving, so I email you soon so that we can keep in touch". "And I really think that you and James should consider Atlanta it would be good for the both of you".

"Thanks Morgan and give my best to your aunts and your grandmother and I hope to hear from you soon".

Mikki turned back to her seat and sat down with her mother in law.

"So what makes you think that you are going to convince my son to move to Atlanta?"

"No one is moving Atlanta, Regina". "I have been approached before about moving to the Atlanta area, but never considered moving because I don't want to be that far away from my family".

"You can take your ole's bourgeois self and your children down to Atlanta but make sure that you leave James here with his real family", Regina hissed.

Just then they both looked up as Terri approached the table with the waiter.

"Oh, Terri, so glad that you could make it this afternoon". "I'd like you to meet James' wife Mikki".

"Nice to meet you Terri", Mikki answered and shook her hand.

"I've heard so much about you Mikki from James and Regina last night".

"So, I've heard". "Well we already ordered because Regina didn't tell me that she had changed our reservations for 3". "But have a seat, I'm more than sure that they will get you a menu and get you started".

"Thanks".

"Well, I am so glad to have my two favorite women, eating lunch with me. Terri, I mentioned Micah to Mikki, did you bring any pictures of him, asked Regina.

"I do, I am so proud of him, he is going to University of Delaware in the fall on full academic scholarship and my family will be close to him because we just purchased a new home in Bear, Delaware".

"That's nice; it seems that you wouldn't be that far from us".

"Oh, really, where do you and James live?"

"He didn't mention that to you last night?"

"No, we were so busy talking about old times that he did not mention that at all". "He did say that we had the same taste in clothes and I have to tell you that I really do like your loafers and your coat is Ann Taylor isn't it?"

"Yes, I love Ann Taylor". "Well, it looks like your food is arriving, that was quick wasn't it?"

The rest of their meal went relatively with just a lot of small talk and when the check came, Terri insisted on paying for the full meal. Regina asked for Terri to drop her off at work, so Mikki was left to herself to make the drive home.

On the drive home, Mikki thought about all that had transpired at lunch, she felt as if she was railroaded with a lot of information but she knew that getting upset and acting a fool was definitely what her mother in law had wanted her to do, but she kept her cool and knew that she would have to talk to James when she got home. She just could not understand why James had not mentioned to her that Micah was his son. She remembered like yesterday, when she had met Terri previously at her wedding to her current husband.

May 1997

Mikki was dressed and ready to go. She was waiting for James to come back with his mother, so that they could go to his old high school friend's wedding. His mother was going to the wedding only, and then they would drop her off at work and head for the reception at Celebrations in Ben Salem. Mikki was a little tired because she was a little over 5 months pregnant with their first child and the summer had came early. She wasn't showing that much which was good and she always felt more comfortable wearing dresses and skirts.

She heard the screen door slam and knew that James was back and it was time to go. She got up off the chaise in the sun room and moved towards the front of the house.

"Mikki, are you dressed and ready to go?"

"Yes, I am coming J, you know I move a little slower than usual, but I am coming!"

"You don't think you are overdoing it by going to this wedding?"

"No, I am fine, I know that they are having a full Mass for their wedding, I just won't get out of my seat because I may have a hard time getting back up!"

"Babe you know that you are the most beautiful pregnant woman, I know, and he kissed her forehead.

"Don't try and butter me up Mr. Stevens, you had a lot to do with this condition and you know that I won't let you forget it".

"Come on Mikki, you had some fun too, he snickered.

"James, come on lets go, I don't want your mom to overheat sitting in your car, because the weather lately has been hot".

"Er, Mikki about my mom, James stammered.

"She's not in the car?"

"Well".

"James, you left here almost an hour ago because your mom wanted to be picked up first and it would be better because we are closer to the church and now she's not here?" " What is going on?"

"Well, my mom had me run some errands for her because she wasn't dressed when I got there". "She said that she forgot what time I told her that I was coming and that if I did the errands for her, that she would be ready when I got back".

"Okay, so why is she not in the car now?"

"When I finished the errands for her, I went back to the house and she said that she needed another ½ hour because she still had to curl her hair".

"J, the wedding starts in less than an hour and we need to get a move on". "So you mean to tell me that you came back to get me and then we still need to drive back to your mom's and pick her up and then drive to Center City to try and make it to St. Peter's Church?" "Are you crazy?"

"Um?"

"You know what don't answer that, this is silly, your mom doesn't drive and it was your suggestion that we all go in one car". "This is your friend's wedding and you are being inconvenienced by all of this driving back and forth". "How about you just go get your mom, make sure she gets to the wedding and pick me up when it's time to go to the reception". "If we don't work it that way, you won't make it".

"Are you sure, babe? You know weddings, never start on time".

Mikki frowned, "J just go and get your mom and make sure that you call me when you are on your way to pick me up for the reception".

Mikki kissed James on the cheek and walked back to the sunroom. It's just easier this way she mumbled to no one in particular.

Mikki had dosed off after James left and realized that he was back when she heard the sliding door to the sunroom open.

"Hey, babe, you ready to go?"

Mikki rubbed her eyes and looked up at James, she noticed that he looked a little frustrated.

"You okay, J?"

"Just a little tired, the reception starts at 6 but I feel like I worked a full day at work".

"You mean all the driving back and forth?"

"Yeah, I mean the wedding was nice, but afterwards, my mom wanted to go and pick up some groceries and she wanted to stop at the Jamaican Jerk Hut on South Street for a takeout plate".

"Did you eat anything?"

"Yeah, I did have a little cabbage and plantains, but I heard that the spread at the reception is going to be really nice, so I wanted to wait, but I wanted to make sure that you and the belly were okay".

"James, I was fine, as you can see, I drifted off sitting back here in the sun room and it's not as hot back here with the ceiling fan".

"Let's get ready to go, I want you to meet Terri and her new husband and some of my friends growing up that you haven't already met". "We need to go and have a good time, but no drinking Mrs. Stevens because you are carrying my baby".

"How about I just stick to water and ginger ale?"

"I'll ask them to put it in a flute for you so you can feel like everyone else who will be drinking champagne".

Mikki popped James on the hand. "Come on Mr. Stevens, we have at least a ½ hour drive to Ben Salem and I heard that I-95 is pretty clear so we better get moving".

During the drive to the reception place in Ben Salem the two of them talked about relatively everything under the sun. James had mentioned to Mikki that they should go and look at a little beach house in Ocean City Maryland. He told her that it would be a good investment and since they liked to visit often because it was a lot quieter than the Jersey Shore they could rent it out in the summer for the weekends that they weren't visiting.

Once they arrived at Celebrations, Mikki was in awe of how nice the grounds looked as well as how big the reception palace was. "James, this place is nice; I know they really had to spend a lot of money to have their reception here!"

"Babe, I know". "I thought that our wedding was over the top but this out did us by leaps and bounds!"

"I'm jealous but I'm not jealous". " You know what I mean?" "Our day was our and was special in every way but this is some old high roller stuff!"

James laughed and when they walked in, he led Mikki in the direction of some people that he knew. "Mikki, I would like you to meet, Eric Jones, the guy that got me kicked out of Boy Scouts".

"Aw, don't believe anything he tells you Mikki, Eric said with a laugh. Eric was a nice looking guy. He was about 6' tall with wavy dark brown hair and light brown eyes. His complexion was the color of café au lait but he had a slender muscular build but had very broad shoulders.

"How's football treating you man?"

"Aw, man you know, I can't call it". " I was on the practice squad with the Eagles for a minute, but I think that if they start this semi- pro league in Trenton, I may go and play with them because it will allow me to do this personal training thing during off season".

"You finally finished your degree?" "Man, I'm proud of you?" "Yeah, well I stopped trying to be a player with the ladies and decided that, although I like playing football and it is giving me a stable income, my knees will give out eventually and I can still help people out by doing personal training". "I am about to start this Master's program because I can learn a thing or two about running my own business".

"I'm proud of you man". "I see they opened the doors for us to go into the ballroom". "How about we go see where we are seated?"

Mikki grabbed both of their arms and smiled, "why not?"

Once they found their name tags in the ballroom, they found out that they were all seated at the same table, not too far from the Bride's mother and step-father. Once they were seated, James went over to talk to the Bride's mother and some of the other family seated at the table with her.

A few minutes later, the bride and groom and their children were introduced because they were the only ones in the party. The bride danced with her husband and then took turns dancing with her sons who from what Mikki saw in the program were 9 and 8 and her new husband danced with their little girl who looked no older than 5. After the dance, the couple danced simultaneously with her stepfather and his mother. With all of the dances out of the way they began serving dinner.

During dinner, Mikki had light conversation with Eric and some of James other friends. "Mikki, did you know that my man James used to be real hot and heavy with the bride", Eric asked.

"No, I didn't, he just said that it was a friend of his from high school".

"Uh, Oh, I guess that omission is going to get you in the dog house! "Don't worry Mikki, if this man right here, messes it up with you, I'll take good care of you", Eric laughed.

"Man, why you always want to get after my women?" "I will not be in the dog house and I told Mikki that it was a young lady's wedding that we were attending". "I didn't let her believe that I knew the guy", he shrugged.

"Well, if they dated in the past and they are not together now, then it must not have meant to be". "However, Mr. Stevens, tell me everything next time and don't let me find out from someone else, okay?"

"Got, it Mrs. Stevens". "I promise not to leave anything else out when giving you information". "Look here comes, the bride and groom coming over to talk to us".

Mikki turned around to see the bride in her stunning off white gown and tiara. She had removed the veil and her train was fasted to the back of her dress so that she would not drag it on the floor. Her makeup was flawless and her hair was done in a French twist with tendril curls around her face.

Once she reached the table she bent over to hug James. "James, I am so glad that you and your wife could make it", she said. "I wasn't so sure after talking to your mom ".

"Terri, I am so glad for you, I see Micah has grown a lot since I last seen you".

"Yes, and although we have moved to Texas due to my husband being in the Air Force, he is doing well in school and has made a lot of friends". "And he also has a brother and sister because my husband and I blended our families".

"Well, I am glad that you are happy Terri". "You really do look good. Terri, I want you to meet my wife Mikki, you'll have to excuse her because she is 5 months pregnant and I want her to take it easy".

"I'll beg your pardon, Mister!" "Hi, Terri it is good to meet you and I just wanted to tell you that you really look beautiful and I am glad that you enjoyed the day".

"Thank you Mikki, if I do say so myself for someone who is almost 6 months pregnant, you are glowing". "And I love that dress!" "So when is your due date?"

"September 15th, but the way this baby jumps around at night, I hope that it comes pretty soon!"

"Well, I haven't been pregnant in about nine years, but I know what your mean!" "Well, I have to say hello to everyone else, I hope that you enjoy yourselves and I am really glad that I met you Mikki". "And do me a favor; make sure you make him learn how to say no".

"Thanks, Terri". Mikki turned to James and asked, "What did she mean by you learning how to say no?"

James shrugged his shoulders and said, "I have no idea".

For the rest of the wedding, James and Mikki enjoyed the music and fun that was part of the splendor of the evening. When Mikki began to complain about her feet, James decided to a call it a night and go home.

James

James knew that Mikki would be home soon, from her outing with his mother and he wanted to get the full spiel on what happened. He had watched the news when him and Mike came back from Oasis with the kids and did not see any report on Action News that a fight had broke out at any Center City restaurants so he knew that his mom had to be on her best behavior and not do anything to rile Mikki up.

Just then his cell phone rang and he walked into the kitchen to get it off the charger. "Hello?"

"James can you please explain to me why that bourgeois wife of yours was hugging on some man when we went to Ms. Tootsies?"

"Mom, what are you talking about?"

"Well, right after we were seated some bozo comes over to the table and starts talking to her about Atlanta, and why she didn't move to Atlanta for the job opportunities". "He was just a smiling all in her face and she was just acting sexy and blinking her eyes and rubbing his hands in front of me!" "It was downright disrespectful!" "He practically begged her to come to Atlanta right in front of me!"

"Mom, why are you calling me making up stuff like this?" "I know that Mikki got a job offer in Atlanta, but she told me that she declined the job offer because she didn't want to move that far away from the families".

"Son she could care less about the families, she couldn't even drop me off at work, Terri happened to be in the area and took me to work to relieve Margie because your wife was too busy being dreamy eyes at this man!"

"Terri took you to work?"

"That's what I said!" "This man name began with an M and she said that they worked together before". "He practically begged her to rethink about moving to Atlanta, and that's when that heifer realized that I was sitting with her at the table, so she decided to introduce me as her friend and not her mother in law". "He was so busy drooling all over her that he didn't care who I was".

"Mom, I think you are getting carried away with this whole story".

"What are you telling me that I am lying to you?" "Son, are you out of your mind?" "I have always had your back and never lied or intentionally misled you in all of your 37years". "I am 54 and I am way too old to play these types of games". "Your wife is thinking about leaving you and I guess she wanted me to be the witness of it this afternoon".

"Okay, mom if that is the truth, why would Mikki agree to go to counseling with me?"

"To make you look like the bad guy and when she divorced you and took those kids, she would be able to get the ½ the money out of the houses, and get some of your retirement money?" "Don't act stupid boy!" "I raised you better than that!" "I told you that women are conniving and misleading". "That is why I always told you family first and I am your family!"

"Mom, I have company and I believe that Mikki is pulling into the garage now". "I will talk to you later".

"Call me tomorrow son, but beware because I warned you!"

James disconnected the call and heard Gina come down the stairs from the guest room. Gina had gotten a little bit bigger since she had announced her pregnancy and had just found out that they were having twins.

"Gina, do you need me to get you anything?"

"No I'm fine, and you know that I am not a guest in your house, if I sit still or lay down any longer, I am going to suffocate!"

"Well, you know that Mike wants you to take it easy right?"

"He is not going to get on my last nerve either by smothering me and chasing me around like a little puppy dog". "We've been through a pregnancy before, although almost 14 years ago, and we will make it through this one".

"Gina, can I ask you a question?"

"Sure, why not?"

"Did Mikki ever talk to you about the job offer that she got in Atlanta?"

"She did, but she wasn't willing to move that far away from your families". "She wanted the children to interact with their grandparents and she didn't think that you would have made the change and what you wanted was most important to her". "Why?"

"Well, I didn't really know about it at first and then my uncle told me about it". "Mikki and I talked about it but with us kind of being in a rocky place right now, I'm not sure she won't pick up and run off it we don't make it over the hump".

"James, I have known Mikki long enough to know that she's not a runner". "She is not explosive and all in your face, she tries to take everyone's feelings into consideration before she speaks". "Part of that is the reason why she is Kyla's godmother, she thought about Kyla and not what Kevin did to her". "She can give people the benefit of the doubt and not hold a grudge, but people also take that as a weakness in her".

"What, that she won't speak up and yell and scream and move her neck around when she thinks you have wronged her?"

"Well that as well as, she tries to give everyone the benefit of the doubt, some try to play her empathetic spirit as weakness". "If you don't do anything else, talk to her, you know your wife and that she is not conniving and secretive". "If she didn't tell you, it wasn't something that she was truly considering".

"Thanks Gina, now let me get the cards and snacks so we can play spades and me and my boy Mike can whip on you and Mikki!"

"I don't man bash, so please just don't cry when we are done killin' you two!" "I am going to check on the kids, they should be occupied with the game in the basement and they already had dinner, so they should be relatively quiet for the rest of the night".

As soon as Gina shut the basement door, the mud room door opened and in walked Mikki. James noticed that she looked a little frustrated but he knew that they would talk about it soon.

"Hey babe, how was Oasis with Mike and the kids?"

"We had fun, Jason showed us all up by climbing up to the very top of the rock wall and the girls won a multitude of tickets on the Wheel of Fortune Game so everyone had a good time".

"Where's Gina?"

"She just went downstairs to check on the kids and Mike is resting his eyes on the couch in my office". "I think that he was snoring too loud when he was lying in the guest room with Gina, so she put him out". "How was lunch with my mother?"

"Very interesting, too say the least, she changed our reservations and Terri showed up".

"What do you mean?"

"Exactly as I said, I made the reservations for 2 under my name and she called and changed the reservations to 3". "About 15 minutes, after we had been seated, Terri shows up at our table to join us". "Once she got there, your mom called us both her favorite women". "I was shocked to hear her say that because when she calls here on the phone, I am little Miss bourgeois".

James raised his eyebrow, "Are you sure that's what happened?"

"What do you mean, James, are you saying that I would lie to you?"

"Well, you didn't tell me about Atlanta until I heard about it from Unc. So what I'm saying is you would leave something out?"

"Okay, I don't know why you would think, I would lie to you but, if that's the case, I could ask you the same thing".

"What do you mean?"

"What I mean is, Terri is back in the area and she just conveniently shows up just before her son's 18th birthday". "Your mom has pictures of him everywhere in her house and not one picture of any of our children". "Last night you come home late and I find out today that you and Terri were at dinner at your mom's last night busting it up and having a good old time". "How soon we forget, that omitting information is just as good as lying James".

"Okay well, what about you fawning all over some guy and talking to him about Atlanta and the job market and forgetting to introduce my mom this afternoon?"

"Oh, so I guess before, I could get home, your dear old mom had to call and give her convoluted version of what happened today?" "Did it ever cross your mind that she was lying to you?"

"My mother would not intentionally lie to me!"

Mikki raised her eyebrows, "Oh and I would?" " James you can go to hell with that notion!" "In our history together, I have always put the children and you ahead of any decisions that I made". "Atlanta was never a decision to be made because our children would have been too far from their grandparents!" "Family is important to me, this family is important to me; I have never ever put anything before you, and never made you feel like you were not the head of the household, never!" "You can't treat me this way anymore, you cannot be the king of two castles, and if you want to believe what that wretched lying woman that you call your mother told you, go ahead". "Go to hell, James, I sure hope you still have that apartment, because you are sure as hell going to need it!" "We are still officially separated and you better get the hell out of my face and my house right now!"

Mikki ran up the steps and James could see the tears that had started to come down her face. He rubbed the back of his head and turned to see his friend Mike stroll out of the office.

"Man, you definitely made a mess of that!" "I overheard you talking to Gina and thought maybe you were okay, but you really picked a big fight with Mikki and for as long as I've known her that is as loud as I've ever heard her get!"

Gina opened the basement door and walked into the kitchen. "Okay what's with the long faces?" "What no more beer in the fridge and no one feels like going for a beer run?"

"No, your boy over here accused Mikki of lying to him, and she told him to get out".

"I'm not playing mediator, my brother, I love the both of you but Mikki would never lie to you about anything!"

"Well, my mom called and said that Mikki was fawning all over this guy at Ms. Tootsies and did not take her to work and that she had to call for a ride".

"Bro, I even know that Mikki is not inconsiderate to just leave your mom stranded". "Anyway, your mom works at 8th and Spruce and Ms. Tootsies is on 13th and South". "She could have walked those few blocks". "Man, you're a bonehead, I know that Mikki only has eyes for you and a lot of men have stepped to her and she shuts them down". "And your mom's told you that she left her?" "Can you really say that you believe that?"

"Let me say it for you, you are a bonehead to the nth degree and I don't know how you are going to fix this one, because again something that your mother did is going to hurt your marriage, and this might be the last straw for Mikki", Gina said.

James just shook his head, and ran up the stairs. He knocked lightly on their bedroom door. When there was no answer, he pushed the door open slightly to see that Mikki was lying on their bed on top of the comforter crying.

"Mikki can we talk?"

"No, I don't want to talk to you James".

"Mikki, please?"

"No, I can't do it". "I have always been on the up and up with you". "Never once have I lied to you". "I may not have told you about the job offer to Atlanta, but I told you that it was never a consideration for me because I loved being close to family". "You have to make up your mind what is most important to you, our family that we created or your mother and her family". "I can't make that decision for you and maybe forcing you to go to counseling wasn't the right idea". "I can't continue to live like this". "I want you to pack your stuff and go back to your apartment, you can have access to the kids at any time but I can't allow you to tear my heart apart with this momma's boy stuff anymore".

"But Mikki, I love you!"

"Do you really?" "Or are you being the upstanding man trying to make everyone happy?" "Part of this is what you want and I have never made you compromise who you are or what you are, I just asked that me and your children be a priority and the time demands that your mother puts should not make us expendable". "Your mom's word should not be the highest of the high and make other's feel inferior". "I have never once made a comparison of you and my father because you were your own man". "I loved you because of your confidence, because of your swagger and part of me respected you because my father always told me that a real man respects and takes care of his mom".

"But your mom is way too dependent on you and you allow her to use you as a crutch". "She has a husband yet, you run to her every beck and call". "Our marriage should be a partnership but sometimes it's not that because I have to hold down the fort because you are doing your mother's bidding". "I refuse to do it anymore, so you need to leave James".

"Mikki, can't we talk this out?"

"No, you have to figure this out on your own, I can't be your crutch". "You also have decision to make where Micah is concerned".

"What do you mean? Micah is not my son."

"Well, your mom sure believes that he is, and I think that part of the reason she invited Terri to lunch was so that they could continue whatever discussion you were having at her house further". "Your mother stated that you and Terri had discussed visitation and that it was time that Micah got to know his father and spend time with him". "Isn't that the reason why you were late coming home from your mom's the other night?"

"Micah is not my son; he is Sierra and Diamond's cousin". "Terri and I discussed me possibly accompanying Micah to see his father in jail". "His father is in Graterford Prison and will be there for the next 25 years before he is eligible for parole". "Babe, we need to work this out and we can't work this out with me moving out again".

"James, I really need my space, I can't do it". "You are not a good multi-tasker, nor do I want to be an item on your multitask listing". "You have stepped on my feelings and my heart multiple times without a second thought of how I feel". "You can spend as much time at the house that you need but I don't want you to sleep under this roof with me until you are fully committed to the whole kit and caboodle without compromising our time with your mother". "I as your wife should feel that I come second to anyone and you have made it quite clear that what your momma's says or needs is the most important and you can just work me in when you can because you know I will compromise and won't be twisting my neck and pointing my finger to get my way". "I am exhausted, so that's where I stand with this whole thing. If you rented out the apartment, you can stay in the guest room once Gina and Mike leave but you are going to need to get another place soon".

James lowered his head and walked out of the room. His wife had told him to go to hell in so many words and he had no one to blame but his self. He knew that Mikki was raging because when she looked him dead in the eye, he did not see one ounce of love for him.

The rest of the weekend went without incident, but Mikki only talked him when necessary. James was concerned that the kids would notice that he and Mikki were not on good terms but he knew not to even dare say anything to her about it. He would just have to see if Brenda could see him earlier on Monday because this was a major crisis.

Monday morning was hell for James; he didn't get any sleep, because he had slept on the couch in his office. The children were excited because Tuesday began their Spring Break and he and Mikki had told them that they could go to their house in Ocean City from Tuesday thru Sunday, because there was going to be a Welcome Spring festival. He worried about how much of a united front that they were going to be able to show the children with him still at home but sleeping in the guest room. He decided that he needed to call Brenda right away to see if she could see him earlier in the day instead of in the afternoon because he really needed to unburden himself.

"Brenda Ratcliff's office, this is Cameron".

"Hi, Cameron, this is Mr. Stevens, is Brenda in early today by any chance?"

"Why, yes she is can you hold on for a minute and I will get her for you?"

"Sure, thanks a lot Cameron".

"This is Brenda, Hi James, how are you today?"

"Brenda, all is not well, I made a mess of things this weekend, and I have been sent back to sleeping in the guest room".

"Well, James I was going to call you because I did speak to Mikki on Sunday afternoon and I feel kind of bad about her assignment that I gave her but I never thought that you two would be at odds behind it".

"It's not your fault, I think my mom had a lot to do with this and I just outright accused Mikki of lying to me and did not take her word".

"Wait a minute, I think I'm missing something, Mikki just told me about another woman showing up at lunch and your mother in law was saying that you were the father of the woman's child". "She never told me about you two getting in an argument". "Look, I want you to tell me the whole story, and I have an open slot at 10:30 if you can get here because this sounds like a crisis".

"I can be there by 10:30, no problem".

"Wait, a minute, Mikki cancelled all of her appointments with me!"

"Brenda, are you sure?"

"I am definitely sure because it was done after she talked to me on Sunday". "I have a voicemail from her thanking me for my time". "This seems so much unlike her".

"No, Brenda, I think I may tell you what happened now between us over the phone before I come to cry on your shoulder at 10:30 but if you said that Mikki has cancelled any remaining appointments that she had with you, that means she has given up on me and I am going to have to fight to get her back".

"Well, I will do whatever it takes to help you James". "Tell me the story of this weekend and then we will work on seeing what I can do to help you".

James began to tell her the whole story of the weekend to only her gasps and uh huhs. When he finished, Brenda advised him that she would look into some things for him and if possible have a game plan for him when he arrived. James hung up the phone but knew that it wasn't going to be an easy fight, but he was ready.

James looked at the clock in his office and realized that it was time to gather his stuff and head over to Brenda's office. He gathered up the work that he had finished on new real estate leads in the area and went out to his secretary's desk to give her the information to file away.

"Amanda, I need to step out of the office for about 2 hours, I have a meeting at 10:30 and will probably be back in the office around 12:30."

"Okay, James but don't forget that Malcolm Scarsborough is coming to meet with you later this afternoon about that retail store in Overbrook that he has an interest in".

"Okay thanks, Amanda, that appointment is for 1:30 and I will be back before then".

James walked out to his car and placed his cell phone and lap top on the passenger seat. He took of his suit jacket and hung that on the back of the chair and got in for the drive to Brenda's office.

Once he arrived, Brenda was at the front desk talking to his receptionist. "Hey Brenda, I am here so please don't slap me so hard on the back of my head". "I got a lot of those from Gina and Mike this weekend, I can't dare take anymore I told you so's".

"I'm not going to tell you I told you so because I have to be impartial, come on let's go back to my office and talk". "I think that if you're willing, I have a game plan that maybe if you work hard and are honest, you may be able to make some headway with your mom and your wife".

They both headed back to Brenda's office where they discussed how he was feeling about the lies from his mother as well as how he felt about seeing Mikki cry and give up on him all in the same day.

"Okay, James, here is what I want you to do, first, I was going to make your session this afternoon, a group session with other men, that I have in the TMBP so that you can meet some of the men that are further along and who this project has been very helpful to". "I still want you to attend that group session, but if you are going to sweep Mikki off her feet in Ocean City this weekend you have to do your part".

"And if this works, will I still have to come to counseling for your research project?"

"How about we just play that by ear, I mean, Mikki was hurting a lot because you were not listening to her". "And from what I know about Mikki, she can shut down when she thinks that people are not taking her feelings into consideration as she would have theirs".

"I know that now, Brenda and if this is the fight of my life, I need to get my wife back even if it means not talking to my mother again".

"I don't think that Mikki doesn't want you to alienate your mother, I think that she just wants more balance than you have given her when it comes to your family and the constraints of your mother".

"I know Brenda, and just like I vowed to love, honor and cherish her, I am going to let her know this week that she is really important to me".

"Well, I know you have to get lunch and be back for your meeting and plan what will take place while you are away, but make sure that you keep your appointment for the Tuesday after you guys come back from your trip to Ocean City".

"I will, and will I see you later at the group session?"

"No my partner, handles those sessions but if there is anything that I need to know, he will give me a call".

"Thanks again Brenda, and please if you get a prayer to a higher power, pray for me because my wife is a stubborn woman!"

Mikki

Mikki was exhausted from packing for their trip to Ocean City. The kids were asleep and James called and said that he would be late but if she was to put all of the luggage and groceries by the door, he would load them when he came in. She looked around to make sure that the kitchen and family room were cleaned and then climbed the steps to go to bed. She was surprised that the children did not question her about James this evening because ever since their big blow up they put up a good front.

Mikki had gotten a call from her lawyer about the legal separation papers and told Mikki that she could come in on Wednesday once they had returned from their spring vacation. Mikki could not understand what was wrong with her, she felt sluggish and all she could attribute it to was all of the stress she was under after her and Mike's big argument. She decided to relax and take a bubble bath but she was going to make sure that she made an appointment with the doctor once she came back from vacation.

Just then she heard the door bell ring and could not understand who would be coming to the house. Her parents were already in Ocean City and they had left earlier this afternoon and she knew that her sisters were going to be there later tomorrow but that they were going to stay with some friends.

"I'm coming! Hold your horses!" Mikki unlocked the top lock on the door and pulled the door open to see her mother in law and Terri standing there.

"Hello, you two, what brings you here at this time this evening?" "Regina, I didn't even know that you knew how to get here if James wasn't driving?"

"Don't get smart with me little Miss Bourgeois, I see your day of reckoning is coming and I plan on delivering it to your personally tonight!"

"Well, with that being said, come in have a seat and tell me what you came for, so you can get out of my house", Mikki said while watching Terri to see what she was doing.

"Terri, can I get you are my mother in law something to drink?"

"No, thank you, I was just asked to drive Regina here over false pretenses, so I don't want to inconvenience you or get into any squabble that you and Regina might have".

Mikki looked at Terri and raised her eyebrow and they both turned to watch Regina walk from the foyer to the family room. They both just shrugged and followed behind her to see what this was going to turn into.

Regina took a seat on the loveseat and Terri sat across from her in the burgundy wing back chair. Mikki sat catty corner from Regina on the couch and twisted her legs underneath her.

"Well, you came here for a reason, so let's get down to business shall we Regina?"

"What I have to say, should be easy for you anyway, because I know after all that fawning you did over that guy when you took me to Ms. Tootsies that you are way too uppity for my son and this charade of a marriage has to come to an end". "My family is falling apart around me, my son has been with you for all these years, and usually girls didn't stick around to long because he always made me the priority". "My daughter won't move back home and my boys are going away to college because they want to be away from me because they don't want me to be dependent on them like I was on James".

"Okay, but what does that have to do with her if you don't mind me asking Ms. Regina", Terri asked.

"James was all I had when people turned their backs on me, his father Jackson wanted his son, but not me, when I got pregnant, my aunt, the woman who swore on my mother's death bed that she would take care of me told me to get out". "So I always hung on to James because he treated me like a queen". "He always changed his plans to make sure that I was safe, he always put me first". "But I can't have that any longer because; Miss Bourgeois and her children need him". "Always looking down her nose at me because, I had James at a young age, always making comments about don't feed the kids that, make sure that you are on time for the kids game, you know we have two houses now we have to make sure that the kids have time for vacation and are well rounded".

"I'm not understanding, why you are upset with Mikki, Regina?" "Any good parent wants that their children do better than them". "You sound like your jealous because James and her work together to do better for your grandchildren".

"James was supposed to be there for me, not walk away or turn his back on me!" "I'm his mother!" "He should be there for only me!"

Mikki was too much in awe to say anything. She thought what she was witnessing was downright crazy. She thought to herself, *she can have James, if I make it out of her safely. I will make sure that those separation papers become* divorce *papers!*

Terri continued asking questions of Regina. "Regina, so you mean to say that you never wanted James to be married, like you are to Russell?"

"Don't get me wrong, I know that Russell loves me, and will take care of me". "But he's just my husband and James is my sunshine that I gave birth to and he is the only one that loves me unconditionally".

"So you believe that if you sabotage his marriage to Mikki, that he will come back to you and be there for only you?"

"Mikki is not good enough for my son". "I raised my son to understand that you could only trust women but so much". "I was the only one that would never lie to him". "I was the only woman he could trust". "But somewhere, I went wrong because he thought about once marrying you Terri, but you messed that up when you got pregnant by someone else". "And then he married this one, at first I thought he was marrying her because he got her pregnant, but their first child wasn't born until September of 1997 almost 18 months after they got married". "I then started to believe that he was infatuated with her because she never complained about rearranging their schedules to accommodate me". "But he never got tired of her, and then I realized that although he loves me as his mom that he had room to love her as well". "We can't continue like that no more". "He has only room to love his mother".

"And why do you think that mom?" "Because you have lied all these years about my father abandoning you and you're selfish?"

All three women looked up to see James standing in the doorway of their family room. Mikki did not move towards him but she could see in his eyes that he wanted her to.

"James, your father did abandon me". "We were in love".

"No mom, you were in love with Jackson, but he had been in a relationship with Chris and Janice's mom for almost 2 years before he met you". "It just so happens that you got pregnant with me". "I'm glad that I walked in on this conversation; it gives me insight on why you act the way you do". " I think you need help mom, and I can't help you with that". "I need to work on getting my family back in order and that means whatever my wife needs me to do to feel safe and that my priorities are straight, I am going to do".

"Son, you really don't mean that you are choosing your wife over me?"

"Yes, I am, she is the mother of my 5 beautiful children, she has always pushed me to be better and to do better". "She really made me the man that I am today because, she just allowed me to be me and not mold me into what she needed me to be". "She just loved me unconditionally". "Your love for me is selfish, it is contingent on what I can do for you, you don't very often give any in return and you need control". "I will be 38 this year, and I need to be devoted to my children and my wife". "So, I will call Russell to come and get you. Terri, I am sorry that you she brought you into this".

"James, actually, I never would have believed it if, I hadn't seen it for myself". "I do have some information on a counselor that may be able to help your mom". "His name is Michael Jamison". "My husband and I have taken his couple workshop when he was in Texas". "He is really good".

"Thanks Terri, I have his information because I am familiar with his partner Brenda".

Terri nodded and headed towards the front door.

Mikki was still in awe about what had just transpired. She still had not said a word and just looked at the frumpled mess that was her mother in law crying on the love seat. She said her good nights to Terri and went to her room. She really was going to need her bubble bath now, but she still wasn't ready to talk to James. Maybe she would set up an appointment to see Brenda when they came back from vacation.

About an hour later, she heard James knock at the bedroom door.

"Yes, James?"

"I wanted to apologize to you for my mother". "I really did not know all of those things until I heard them come out of her mouth this evening". "When I went to the seminar with Mike Jamison, some of the other gentlemen had discussed that as well and I am really starting to believe that I can benefit from the TMBP sessions so that I can be a better husband and overall better to myself as a man. I hope that we can work on us Mikki". "I would hate to lose you and what we have, I meant everything that I said about you".

"James, I'm glad that you understand your mom now, but I think that you may be better off, being by yourself, so that you can understand what you want. I don't want to force you to be with me and the children". "And if you can only be a good dad, I can accept that right now". "I can't say that right now, I am willing to give you a chance to hurt me again". "I can't give you the benefit of the doubt, because when I really needed you, you left me high and dry". "Let's just have a good vacation with the kids and maybe we can talk when we get back".

"Mikki, I have to tell you that you are being stubborn, and I see that you have a wall up where I am concerned". "But I am determined to show you that you are my everything".

Mikki yawned, "Well we need to be on the road by eight, because that will give us enough time to travel and get settled at the house before 11 am". "That way we can feed the children lunch before taking them to the *Ripley's Believe it or Not Museum*". "This will be a good vacation for the children and just time to relax". "I think that my parents will have a good time spending some time with the kids as well".

"Mikki do you feel okay, you look a little grey around the gills?"

"J, I really think I am just a little stressed, so I plan on taking some Brenda Jackson and Adrianne Byrd novels with me to read, when the kids are taking naps". "I think this vacation is going to do me some good as well".

"Well, good night, I will probably be up before you, so I'll see you in the morning".

"Good night J".

The next morning, Mikki felt a bit nauseous, but shook it off quickly, the children had baths the night before, and so she just had to make them brush their teeth, and wash their faces and allow for them to get dressed. When she got downstairs, she saw that James had packed the last bit of things in his truck and was working on putting jackets on Jason and the twins and reminding Steven and Scott to make sure that they had the videos that they wanted to watch in the car.

She walked in the kitchen to go in the refrigerator and grab her bottle of V8 splash and an apple. "Good morning, James". "Are we all ready to go?"

"Yes we are all ready to go and I just wanted to let you know that I made arrangements for you to go to the spa this afternoon, your parents are going to meet me and spend the day with the children at the museum". "I told mom and dad that you were looking a little stressed so they were happy to chip in".

"That's nice of you James, but I didn't mind going to the museum with the children."

"I know Mikki, I just think you need to have a spa day and the kids will be fine".

"Okay, but don't make any more decisions for me about this vacation okay?"

"Okay, Mik, don't tear my head off, I was just trying to be nice". What she didn't know was he had plans to woo her big time while they were away. He was planning to win his wife back come hell or high water!

"Okay guys, let's all load up in daddy's truck so we can get on the road". "Grandma and Pop- Pop will be joining you guys at the museum". "So we need to get to the house have lunch so that you can have a fun afternoon".

"Yeah!", They all screamed in unison.

James followed the children out to the car and Mikki did one final last check to make sure that all things were turned off in the house. She picked up her Burberry Diaper Bag that had all of the things that the children would ask for while in the car and turned off the kitchen light and headed to the garage so that they could get on the road.

About, two hours later when they were pulling up at their house in Ocean City, she saw that her parents were already waiting for them. James maneuvered his Sequoia into the driveway and pushed the button for garage door. Mikki turned around to see that Skylar, Shannon and Jason were fast asleep in the back seat and Steven and Scott were playing games on their game boys.

Once James stopped the car, Mikki helped the children get out of the car and into the house so that they could have lunch and get unpacked. Since it was only 10:45, she would have time to make lunch and then head to her spa appointment that James had set up for her. She reminder herself to make sure that she tell him thank you again but, she didn't want him to get his hopes up about her changing her mind about what she said. She was determined to protect herself from James going forward.

Mikki looked up to see that her parents were in the kitchen drinking coffee. She thought that it was odd, because although her parents had keys to the house, they had never used them before.

"Hey, Mom and Dad". "I knew that you were going to the museum with the kids, but I thought that James was just going to meet you there?"

"Hello, daughter dear, we were in the area and decided we would be here when you arrived". "We decided that we were going to kidnap the children and James and give you some time to go to the spa", her father stated.

Her mom continued, "Yes, Sweets, we were worried about you". "When I talked to James last night he told me that you looked quite tired and stressed". This is a vacation; you need a break from the children and some vacation time for you".

"Okay, who are these people and what have they done with my parents?" "Am, I missing something?" "Are you two going through some type of mid life crisis?"

Her father laughed, "Sweets, we have spent time with the grandkids and we can handle them, we raised our own brood". "Trust me we will be fine". "I see that the car has pulled up to take you to the spa, so get your purse and get going".

"Car? Who is taking me to the spa?"

"James walked up behind Mikki, "I ordered a car, so that you will not have to drive". "I just want you to enjoy your day of rest and relaxation and your parents and I will make sure that the kids are okay". "Be a lady of leisure today".

Mikki raised her eyebrow at James and then looked over at her parents, "Okay, I will go and enjoy myself, but I will see you guys for dinner".

"Bye, have a good day", they all said in unison.

Mikki grabbed her purse and walked out the door shaking her head.

James

Once he knew that Mikki was at least down the block, and that the children were in the family room watching cartoons, James went into the kitchen to talk to his in-laws.

"Okay, mom and dad, this is what I have planned for Mikki today". "Dad, I know you know some of what transpired in the last couple of days and mom you know what happened last night, but I have to do it big, if your stubborn daughter is really going to listen to me and give me a chance".

"James, my daughter is more than stubborn and she can really hold a grudge when she's hurt". "She get's that mean streak from her father". Anyway, I know you really love my daughter and are willing to fight for her, but I can definitely tell you that it's going to be rough!"

James laid out the day for his in-laws, the day was filled with so many things for Mikki to do and he could only hope that he would cap off the night with Mikki at the Inn on the Ocean. James packed the children up in his Sequoia along with his in-laws and then got his keys to their car so that he could complete the errands that he needed to make sure that Mikki had the time of her life today.

Mikki

Mikki had enjoyed herself, at the Grand Spa. She felt refreshed and her facial was divine. She saw that the driver was back to pick her up, and when she looked at her watch it was way after two and she knew that she would be able to make it to meet her family at the museum. She climbed into the backseat of the car and asked the driver if he could drive her over to the Ripley's museum.

"Sorry, Mrs. Stevens, I have instructions to make sure that you are a lady of leisure and you are well relaxed for this evening".

"This evening, what are you talking about?"

"I was given an itinerary and your next stop will be for a late lunch at *Olive Tree Restaurant*".

"What itinerary?"

"Mrs. Stevens, I can't divulge a lot of information but, while you lunch, I have to run to the mall and pick up the selection of clothes that were purchased for you to view and when you are done lunch, I am to deliver you to *Inn on the Ocean* where there are instructions to make sure that you go directly to your suite". "If at any time you feel that you do not want to continue with the day planned for you, I will return you to your home".

"I guess that I can just enjoy myself for today, I don't always get pampered like this!" " Why not? It won't hurt to be a lady of leisure for one day."

"Okay then, Mrs. Stevens, off to Olive Tree", the driver said.

Once they arrived at Olive Tree, the driver advised Mikki that she had to wait in the car until he went in and advised them that she had arrived. The driver returned and escorted her to a private table where a bouquet of star gazer lilies awaited her.

"Mrs. Stevens, you don't have to worry about placing an order, because you lunch has been especially selected for you". "Take your time having your lunch and I will be back to pick you up at 4".

"Thanks and I will see you then". "I don't know what James is up to, but I will go along with it to see how the day turns out". "I see that James is pulling out all the stops, but I also like that I have the option to say stop.

The waiter arrived at Mikki's table with a piping hot order of zucchini sticks and a carafe of wine. "Mrs. Stevens, my name is John and I will be your server today". "First we have the wine selection for you today is one of the house favorites, *Leone de Castris Salis Salentino* it is a wine from the lower part of Italy". "If you need anything, just let me know". "Your entrée will be out in about 10 minutes".

"Thanks John". *Okay, I need to pinch myself,* Mikki thought. James ordered me a nice Italian Wine, zucchini sticks instead of bread sticks and left my favorite flowers for me?" "If this is a dream and I am still laying on the table getting my massage, just let me be!"

As the rest of the meal progressed, Mikki began to relax a little bit more and just enjoy the ambiance of her surroundings. Her entrée came and she knew that James was really doing it up big. Her entrée was *Fettuccini Fruit De Mere* which had all of her favorites, jumbo lump crab meat, shrimp and scallops served with a crème sauce. *"James, really knows me well. Maybe, I am being a little harsh on him. He can't control his mother, but he sure doesn't have to always be so accommodating. I think that I will call Gina and talk to her".* Mikki took her cell phone out of her purse and dialed Gina's number but got no answer. "Hum? I wonder why Gina's not answering her phone? She usually picks up on the second ring". Maybe, I should call Michelle, she is always willing to tell me off and tell me how stubborn, I am. Mikki dialed Michelle and got no answer. She then dialed Brenda because she knew that she hadn't talked to her since Monday and she at least owed Brenda an explanation as to why she cancelled all the rest of her sessions. "This is getting crazy, I need to talk to my friends and no one is answering!

The waiter came over and cleared her dishes away and advised her that dessert would be out soon. "Thanks, John", Mikki answered with a sad smile. She twirled the last of her wine in her glass and looked around the restaurant. "What am I going to do about James? I am still hurting and I definitely don't want to go to that hotel if I am not willing to work it out right now".

Just then John returned to the table and added three plates and three wine glasses.

Mikki looked up and asked, "Will there be people joining me?"

"Yes Ma'am, this is part of your itinerary, the ladies joining you will be right in, your driver went to pick them up as well". "Dessert will be right out and I will be bringing you a dessert wine as well".

"Thanks, John, I will make sure that you get a big tip".

"No, need ma'am, the gratuity has been already taken care of".

"There she is over there guys".

Mikki looked up to see the three people who she had just been trying to call. Brenda, Gina and Michelle walked over to her table.

Mikki smiled and stood up to greet all three. "I guess, James put you all on my itinerary today so that you can read me the riot act as well?"

"No honey, we are here because we love you and we want you not to be hurting at this time", Gina said.

"Well, I'm not going to be all that nice about it, I'm just going to give it to you straight!" "Cuss that man out, give him hell and then make up with him!" "Girl you look miserable", Michelle said.

"Why thanks, just tear my head off!", Mikki responded.

"Look, Mikki what I think we all are trying to say is that you shouldn't be giving up on James". "His mom wants you to give up on your marriage and in her own demented way she would have won", began Brenda. "Girl, I know that I am your counselor, but we have become friends over the time that you have been coming to me, and you know that you play a role in this whole Momma's Boy thing that James is going through". "You know that I have been doing research for a good long time on this phenomenon, and you are not one of the cases where I would say it can't be fixed". "James really loves and respects you and I think the icing on the cake was to hear what his mother had to say to you and what the other men in the program had to say to him about changing their situations".

"I know your right, Brenda but I can't change my feelings about having to compromise for his mother and the things that James does can be done by his step-father or his brothers".

"Girl, get yourself together!" " Get a backbone or something!" "But stop whining about something that James is trying to correct". "You always get on our case about forgiveness and giving others the benefit of the doubt, why can't you do that in this situation with James?" Michelle asked.

"Whoa Michelle, aren't we a little grouchy today, Gina said. "Look Mikki, if you can forgive others, you have to be willing to forgive James". "James in some ways from the information that I got from Brenda is a minor player in this whole situation". "She believes that James has a grasp on what is important and I think all of what he is going through today is his way of proving it to you". " Wait, here comes the waiter with the dessert and my cranberry juice".

The waiter comes back with dessert lasagna which is enough for all to share and places cranberry juice in front of Gina.

"Excuse me John, can I get a glass of cranberry juice as well, I can't drink the wine. Thank you".

The other three woman turn to look at Michelle because they knew, as far as wine was concerned, Michelle always drank wine when they did and she had a good collection of wines at her home.

"Okay, what gives Michelle? You're not drinking wine? Gina asked.

"Well, if you must know guys, I just found out that I am 8 weeks pregnant, so I can't partake in the wine festivities today".

"Congratulations, Michelle but who may I ask is the father of the baby? We know that you haven't been dating anyone because you work so much".

"Well, I haven't told him yet but because I am with my friends, I will tell you that it's Zavier". "We have been seeing each for a year now but because he is still based out of New York a lot of the times, I would be there with him or he would sneak in for the weekend and stay at my house".

"Michelle, I am so happy for you!" "But why all the sneaking around? You and Zavier have known each other for years", Gina quipped.

"Well, yes we have known each other for years because he is friends with James". "But I wasn't sure about him initially". "I did not know what his intentions were and also, he has a daughter with a former girlfriend who is very demanding, I wasn't sure that it was going to work with us".

Mikki laughed, "Okay, Zavier doesn't fit your list of what you in a man that you date". "Let me see, can't have any baby mama drama, has to work, must be honest etc, etc, etc". "What happened to that he is genuine and can just be a friend to you?"

"Look, I know that I had issues about men because of I believed happened between my parents". "But, I have gone to counseling and I found out that it was me that needed to forgive my dad as well as my mom because as her child, she should have never divulged any information to me about their relationship because I was oblivious to it otherwise". "My father was always good to me and I had the ability to watch him with my siblings and see that people make mistakes and we need to get over them".

"Wow, those are some good revelations from you but, look at the time we have to have Mikki make a decision because, she needs to meet James at *Inn on the Ocean* by 6 and she needs to get dressed with the clothes in the car, Brenda said.

"Well, are you going to join your husband for a night away from the kids, to talk and tear up the separation papers? Gina asked.

"Yes, but I need your help with one thing before I go to meet James". She whispered to all three what she needed to get and they all slapped hands and told her to get her stuff and then headed to the car.

James

James paced nervously around the room. Mikki was late. He tried calling Brenda, Michelle and Gina but got no answer from any of them. He called back to the house and his mother in law said that Mikki was not there. If everything was going to work the way he planned, Michelle and Gina were supposed to be at the house to relieve his in laws and stay with the kids until him and Mikki checked out of the hotel tomorrow morning.

"Please let her be on her way here and nothing happen to her", he thought. Just then, the phone to his suite rang and he could only hope that it was the front desk telling him that Mikki had arrived. "Hello, yes this is Mr. Stevens". "Okay, I will be right there". James grabbed his card key and rushed out of the door.

Once he got to the front desk, James was told that there was a mix up with his delivery and that he needed to sign for something that was sent in its place. James was a little frustrated because he really needed the Haribou Gummi bears but instead he had Gummi Savers.

Mikki really loves that brand, I was trying to recreate how I proposed to her.

"Excuse me, do you know where I can get some Gummi bears? "I really need to get Gummi Bears and not what was delivered for me", James asked the gentleman behind the front desk.

"Mr. Stevens, I believe that you may want to check in the gift shop there may be some in there".

"Thanks, I'll check there".

James walked in the direction of the gift shop not noticing Mikki walking in from beach entrance.

After finding another brand of Gummi bears, James headed back to the room. *"I really hope that Mikki is here"*, he thought, *"I just could not bear that she did not show up"*.

When he got to the room, James put the key into the door and opened it to see that the French doors were open and he knew that he did not leave them open. He walked towards the door to see that Mikki was standing on the balcony looking out at the beach. He noticed that she had on the dress that he purchased for her but was barefoot. On the table, she had his favorite drink, *Bailey's Crème Caramel*, two martini glasses, ice bucket and martini shaker. He moved towards her hoping that he wasn't imagining seeing her there, especially because she was late.

"Mikki?"

She turned around and he could see the tears in her eyes. "I thought you finally gave up on me, James".

"I would never do that Mik, I just went to the front desk because something that I ordered for you did not arrive, and we may have just missed each other".

They both moved to each other and when James reached her he pulled her into his arms and kissed her forehead. He then kissed her hands and her neck and then both cheeks.

"Mikki, I see you brought gifts for me, but I have something in the bedroom for you". "I know that you are still unsure of me, but I want this to be the beginning of me proving to you that you and the children are my main priority". "The children, I believe know that because you and I make them feel important and loved, but I think I need to let you know that you are the love of my life and not even my mom is going to come in between us again".

"James, I know that but it has been very stressful time lately and I don't want to make you feel that I'm ungrateful, but when your mom takes advantage of you, it affects me because I love you".

"Shh, Mikki open the door to the room and I want you to see what I have for you".

Mikki opened the door to see that on the bed was a red and white table cloth with a picnic basket that was filled with Chocolate Cherries, Soft Pretzels, Tastycake Chocolate Juniors and Lemon pies, Herr's ruffled plain potato chips, French Onion Dip, Raspberry Truffles and Cran-Grape juice. Next to the picnic basket was a picture of the two of them together from when they went on the ski trip for his birthday and a picture from their wedding with her looking down at him on bended knee. There was a note attached to basket but it was folded so Mikki was unable to read it.

"Go ahead Mikki, please read the note", James said.

Mikki moved closer to the bed and sat down next to the basket and removed the note. James moved closer and got down on one knee in front of her so that he could hand her a handkerchief because he could see that she had began to cry.

"Mikki, don't cry baby, here let me read what it says to you so that you can give me an answer". He removed the letter from her hand and began to read. "Mikki, I love you with all my heart, you are my best friend and I would never want something that my mother is going through to sever our relationship". "I am laying everything that I am as a man down so that you can see that, I am making changes to show you, that you are the only one for me". "I will do whatever it takes, even if it means continuing to be part of TMBP and going to counseling to prove that as the minister said when we got married, What God Put Together let No Man break up!" " I hope that you can forgive me and allow me back in your heart as your husband, James".

"J, I love you and I know that I have been stubborn but a lot of what we have gone through has been very overwhelming for me, and when you wouldn't talk to me about decisions that you had made or when I thought that I had pushed you too far with going to counseling and my ultimatum, I just figured that you were done". "Often, when you don't talk to me or tell me what is going on, I get upset because we talk about everything and I felt like you were shutting me out".

"Mikki, I didn't know how to talk to you about my mom". "I knew for a long time that she was a burden to me and that I enabled her to be that way, but I didn't know how to fix it". "It was hard for me to talk to you about it, because in some ways, I felt like I failed you because I wasn't giving you my all like I knew that I should". "You tolerated a lot from my family, but mainly my mom and she took that for a weakness in you, but I always saw it as strength because it is harder to just walk away than to cuss somebody out or to fight at the time you've been attacked".

"I know we are going to get through this but what are you going to do about your mom?"

"Mikki, that is not my concern, yesterday, I spent a lot of time with other men, who are going through some form of drama that has been forged by their relationships with their mothers". "Brenda also arranged for me to talk to Russell and he needs to handle that going forward. My mother has a loving husband and if that marriage is going to survive, she had to work with Russell to figure that out".

"Okay, I'm glad to hear that but I'm hungry and I need to have some of those truffles out of that basket".

James laughed, "Mikki, you can't be hungry you had a big late lunch today!"

"I didn't say that I was hungry but I saw the truffles and the chocolate cherries, and I just have to have some!" "Go and get the Bailey's and we have a chocolate fantasy party".

"Okay, I'll grab the Bailey's and the ice bucket and glasses and I couldn't find the right brand of Gummi Bears for you so I got these from the gift shop". He handed her the Gummi Savers and the Gummi Bears and then walked out of the room.

When he returned to the room, Mikki was curled up under the blanket and had removed her dress and was fast asleep. He kissed her on her forehead and decided to let her sleep because she really looked exhausted.

Mikki

Mikki opened her eyes and lifted her head to check where she was. She noticed that James was not lying next to her and it felt like he had never lain in that spot. She jumped out of bed and grabbed the robe that was laying on the chaise to go and look for James.

When she opened the door, she saw that James was lying on the couch in the sitting area in his pajamas with the newspaper in his lap. She walked over to him so that she could place a kiss on his forehead like he often did her and as soon as she did he reached up and grabbed her and pulled her into his lap.

"Gotcha! You thought that I was asleep didn't you?" "I heard you moving around in the suite so I decided to fake like I was sleeping".

"James, that is not funny! Did you at least get some rest?" "I see that I fell asleep on you last night".

"I figured that you were tired, from the stress and just needed to relax babe". "But breakfast will be here soon, and we have to check out by noon". "So why don't you go and get in the shower and get ready and then we can just relax together before we go relieve the troops with the kids".

"How about I wait and you join me?"

"Sounds good to me, Mrs. Stevens". James followed behind Mikki into the bedroom and then into the shower.

Epilogue

"We would like to introduce you to our new part time staff that will be working with us on the TMBP dissertation". "James Stevens, will work as our new intake coordinator, Steven Choice will serve as one our counselors and Gregory Black will also serve as one of our counselors". "Please give them all a round of applause".

Mikki clapped along with all of the families in attendance at the small reception that was being held at the Petite Ballroom of the Ritz Carlton. Mikki was proud of James and the transition that they made with handling the demands of his mother. She was also glad that Brenda and her team had made this a family affair where she could bring the children.

James and Brenda walked over to where Mikki stood. "Hey Mik, how did you like everything?", Brenda asked.

"Brenda, everything was very nice and I am so happy that you got funding to continue to help families and men in need".

"Well, James will be an asset as well to us continuing to help people". "I am just glad that you two are back on track". "I couldn't wish more happiness for anyone else". "I see you're starting to show as well, how do you feel?"

"Well, I am over the morning sickness, and my feet haven't started swelling so we should be smooth sailing from now on". "We are due in November, so suffice to say, I was pregnant during spring break and didn't know it but this will be the last Steven's child if I can help it!"

"She got that right, Brenda!" "We are going to have to sell our house or add some rooms on!"

The three of them laughed.

Discussion Questions

1. Did you relate to any characters in the book? If yes, who and what made you relate to that character.

2. Do you think that Mikki was right for always getting upset about James's mother situation?

3. Did you expect that Rita would ever change her behavior and the way she acted towards Mikki?

4. As mothers, sometimes we invest a lot in our children and their success; do you think that was the case with Regina?

5. Why do you think that Russell was upset with James?

6. Were you surprised in the change in Rita?

7. Do you think that Mikki was too forgiving at times?

8. When Mikki finally gave up and wasn't willing to talk to James after he accused her of lying, did you think she was acting like a spoiled brat?

9. Why do you think that others could see that Regina was taking advantage of James and he couldn't?

10. Do you think sometimes parents raise their children to be what they want them to be? And was Regina guilty of this?

About the Author

Alexandria is a Philadelphia native that currently resides in the suburbs of the Philadelphia area with her family. She enjoys reading, writing, shopping, community service and hanging with her family and friends. She currently works for a major insurance company in Provider Relations. You can contact her via email @ naiyellem@yahoo.com.